Pebbles on the Sea-Shore

S.K. Narang

Published by
Ocean Books (P) Ltd.
4/19 Asaf Ali Road,
New Delhi-110 002 (INDIA)
e-mail: prabhatbooks.com

ISBN 978-81-8430-564-7
PEBBLES ON THE SEA-SHORE
by S.K. Narang

Edition
First, 2019

Price
₹ 450.00 (Rupees Four Hundred Fifty only)

Printed at
R-Tech Offset Printers, Delhi

Pebbles on the Sea-Shore

Pieces of Pebbles

...My gown became a subject matter of ridicule and mockery in the home and generated a lot of amusement and laughter at times... grave political conditions, supplemented by spiraling mob-violence, gripped the whole nation... Instead of living peacefully as human beings with love, with generosity, and without violence, we resort to hatred, brutality and antagonism.

Stolen glances thus exchanged began to convey more than words and love began to blossom silently but rapidly... Life should be big, may not be long and, as a soldier, I should face the bullet on my chest and not on my back...Gurdeep would come back one day to take her Channi to join him in eternal peace in the celestial abode.

Let me confess, I am a very bad character and don't want my son to follow in my footsteps...It will surely rain tonight and by the morning, even the foot-marks will be lost in the expected rain. It is a golden opportunity...Truth ultimately triumphs. It can be hidden but not defeated. Solutions to some problems should be left to time. Remember, life doesn't go on our terms, rather we go on life's terms.

Children have a tendency to live in the world of make-shift belief and wanted me to purchase a house by mustering money from 'somewhere' which their innocence could neither define nor suggest...The challenge for a democracy is not that it will change devils into angels. Its peculiar dignity is to get even devils to do the right thing.

He now felt guilty of withholding the secret of his marriage and birth of the baby...could never summon enough courage to stand against the pernicious and unjustified demands of his greedy wife and meekly surrendered... dishonouring of cheques and piling up of cases in courts... Balance is essence of all actions in life...Strive to be balanced, rise above all dualities.

...choice of career should be the result of a collective thought-process... Parents don't set limits. Children define their own. Give strength to their wings...They will trace and explore their own skies...Live in the present and let the worries of the future not destroy the pleasures of the present.

My instinctive feeling is that he is hiding something... The sordid scene of violent pushes by the plain-clothed policemen and some fist-fight was witnessed by the shocked and outraged public...because of legal complications... one may get only dates and frustration...the dreams and aspirations of many a young lover are crucified at the cruel hands of social, economic, caste...and religious barriers.

A few drops more and the man moved his hands...tears of joy spattered in his eyes...no act of kindness, howsoever small, is ever wasted...unable to express himself due to language... curious is the dynamics of love...pain of separation...only the sufferer can realise...I love her...as my god.

I did push him into the shallow waters on the sea-shore but never with the motive of killing him...There is no greater punishment than the realisation of one's mistake... But you never murdered me. I am alive. ...Once she wanted to be out of the murky jail and cursed the day she was thrown in, today she wanted to stay in the jail with John but was being pushed out.

Contents

1
The Patched Gown

"You cannot save money by spending it" was an invaluable piece of advice that my late grandfather gave me when I very reluctantly relinquished the strong family bonds and was pushed into wilderness in search of livelihood. Like an obedient child, I religiously stuck to this unique inheritance throughout my life. With age, the immortal words dug deeper and deeper into my heart. I was always averse to being prodigal and something literally paralysed my hands while taking money out of my pocket for an avoidable expenditure. Unlike many others who embark upon an evasive expenditure and remain mentally disturbed long afterwards, I would always ask myself beforehand, "Can this expenditure be avoided? Do I need it or do I want it?" A 'need' would not be delayed but a 'want' would be certainly postponed. I always prayed to God to fulfill my need but not the greed. This nature of mine had shielded me from the woeful cruelty of many a social Shylocks and the savings had helped me to retain something for the rainy day. To avoid getting into a trap, I developed an aversion for borrowing money and always lived within my means. In fact, both borrowing and lending, I believed, invariably created a dent in relations and getting entangled in the web of dues and debts was always avoided.

For these habits, I was often dubbed as a miser and frequently bullied by my wife and children. Unfortunately, they never backed my views on money matters. They could not appreciate the value of money which was, for me, god on earth. Whatever was slightly out of fashion would be immediately discarded by them. Their so-called modern life style and socially approved necessities were sheer extravaganzas in my rarely asked for opinion. In my limited fixed salary, my children were not prepared to cut their coat according to cloth, for this never conformed to their philosophy of life. There was a wide generation gap where age hesitated and youth was reckless. My wife, though not arrogant, was always dominant and would finally manage her say. Right from the very first day of our chance-meeting and resultant love marriage, I played the role of a second fiddle and, thus, committed the blunder of mutely yielding to her and allowing her to have an upper hand in all major decisions. In the garb of modernity, my children viewed my age-old worldly experience as primitive and decayed. We were always on a collision course whenever they forced me to cough up some money that burnt a hole in my pocket. I had simply to flutter and fume within myself for fear of ridiculous remarks from all quarters. Silence was my best defence even if it was taken as a weakness. However, their frequent harassment and bitter criticism could never impact my basic nature.

Though there were no parallels, I was at times bracketed with a maternal uncle of my wife who was blamed for being conservative and for possessing futile and rigid thoughts. He lost his wife immediately after his marriage, leaving no heir to his vast empire. He was ever careful to retain even waste papers, wrappers, empty cardboard cartons and pieces of cloth. "You do not know how useful these are in times of need" was his oft-repeated justification. His instinct of possession and queer characteristic behaviour were proverbial in wider family circles. He won't hesitate to put patches of odd clothes and would never wear a new set of clothes unless given as gift by someone. Instead of appreciating the generosity of the giver, he would mock at him for being spendthrift. He left a huge fortune for his worthless nephew to be enjoyed for generations. These and other identical illustrations had a temporary effect on me but in the face of a stimulus, my responses invariably coincided with my natural habit.

Long back I had purchased a much-needed woolen gown from a pavement shop run by a Tibetan refugee on The Mall in Simla. The memorable treasure had been acquired by me from the savings reaped out of the entitled allowances by staying with a friend during an official visit. The bargain, struck after tremendous exploration and haggling, had been highly appreciated by all. The gown, though cheap and course, was a prized possession and an ever faithful companion during the bone-chilling winters. It had adequately compensated for other clothes which I would have normally purchased for daily use in the home. I wished it to last longest but like all perishable things, it also had a pre-determined span of life. In just about a dozen years, it was torn above the right shoulder due to normal wear and tear. The silken waist cord had already been replaced by a common cotton cord. The faded colour and the absence of any trace of wool on the gown bore ample testimony to its continuous long use and distinguished faithful service. I was still not prepared to part company with it, not for any emotional bond, as would be normal with many, but due to the fact that replacement would cost me an additional fortune which I was not prepared to part with.

In course of time, my gown became a subject matter of ridicule and mockery in the home and generated a lot of amusement and laughter at times. It was described as an antique piece worthy of decorating the shelves of National Museum or fit for display in an international exhibition where it may fetch a million dollars for my descendents after a century. All would join hands in a tirade against me but I would not display any emotional retaliation. I was determined to repair the damaged gown rather than buy another one.

Unwilling to part company with my proud possession, I decided to put a patch on the damaged shoulder, rather than discard it, give it in charity or exchange it for a utensil. The first effort was to find a piece of cloth of a similar colour so as to avoid criticism or any social mockery. The effort having failed, I decided to mend the gown with a piece of cloth of a matching colour. My wife refused point blank to help me in doing such a ridiculous job and be a part of my enterprise. My determination was equally firm where money was involved. Knowledge of sewing and needle-work, gained under compulsion in a few periods during student life, came to my rescue. On a Sunday evening, there was a god-sent opportunity. All were busy enjoying a movie on TV and none was there to display a visible reaction or sarcasm on my adventure. I repaired my gown with course stitches and proudly exhibited my achievement to all. Their sinister silence naturally convinced me of their approval.

In the evening, while I was coming back from my office on foot, my eyes casually fell on an old man sitting on a brick-platform under a big banyan tree. I had often seen him sitting cross-legged on that platform. With small children, there was an atmosphere of fun and laughter as he played, danced and cut jokes with them and with older and mature audience, he was normally deeply engrossed in some serious discussion. Men, women and children, affectionately called him *'baba'*. I did not know much about him except that he was a gentle soul, a refugee from West Pakistan and had none to look after him. People of the area were indeed kind to him and would voluntarily offer him meals and meet his other needs. On that evening, as a matter of routine, I had just passed when my legs suddenly held me back. I stopped for a fraction of a second and glanced at the old man. He was wearing a gown that appeared to be quite familiar. I retraced my steps and as he turned his right shoulder towards me, I was quite sure that it was my patched gown. I was furious but hesitated to retaliate without proper investigation. I was, however, convinced that my eyes could not have erred in identifying my precious asset. I virtually ran back home and dashed straight to my bedroom. In my anxiety to locate my gown, I threw all my clothes on the bed. To my utter dismay, it was missing.

During this entire venture, my wife had perhaps been keenly observing the whole drama. Suddenly, I realised that someone was sneaking on me and on looking back, I found my wife casually leaning against the door with an unusual smile on her face.

"What are you looking for?" she asked with apparent innocence.

"Where is my gown?" I could not control my emotions and thundered, lowering the stress on the last part of the sentence when I saw her raising her eyebrows and staring at me like a disturbed tigress.

"How do I know about your things? It must be where you had left it in the morning," she replied with a casual smile on her face.

"I had hung it here on the peg."

Absolutely unconcerned about my anxiety, she turned her back and went straight to the kitchen. I stood speechless for a few seconds and followed her while trying to rehearse in my mind the words that I wanted to say.

"Look! Don't try to hide the truth. I saw...an old man... wearing the same," I said emphatically after mustering the needed courage.

"I don't understand what you say." There was apparently no seriousness in her behaviour and I was shocked at the ease with which she was posing ignorance.

Refusing to drop my resolve, I repeated, "The old man who sits under the banyan tree and is known as '*baba*' seemed to be wearing my gown."

"I have no idea...You are supposed to look after your belongings." She still maintained the same sinister smile and a look of absolute casualness on her face. My annoyance and emotional reaction did not create an iota of impact on her. This highly infuriated my already agitated mood.

"Don't test my patience. There is something mischievous in your eyes. Your words can hide the truth but not your eyes. Tell me the truth." There was firmness in my words.

"I have given it to him," she replied with the authority of a dictator, laying all possible stress on "I". The whole conspiracy of which I was unaware, I guess, was perhaps hatched on that morning or the previous night.

Pouring tea in two cups and bringing them to the dining table, she continued with a challenge. "Do you want to know anything more?"

I was completely taken aback and felt much offended at her unilateral decision but could not have the courage to say anything except "You should at least have asked me before giving it to anyone...Don't you think that would have been better?"

Pushing the much desired cup of tea towards me and conveniently ignoring my concern, she continued, "Come on dear, take some tea. You seem to be very tired today...I will explain everything to your satisfaction."

Taking a sip of tea, she tried to play on my emotional weakness and glanced at me through the corner of her eye with a teasing smile. "I did not ask you for two important reasons," she resumed. "Firstly, I don't think it is necessary to take your permission for such a trivial matter. It was a shame to wear such an old, torn and useless piece of cloth. You should be thankful to me for relieving you of such a disgraceful thing."

I was completely speechless and sat dumb-founded like a statue. Her justification showed an absolute disregard for my bruised feelings. Taking pity on my failing courage, she was kind enough not to hurt my sentiments anymore and continued with extreme politeness, "I have saved some money and shall buy a new gown for you."

A little silence, and she continued, "You haven't asked me about the second reason?"

Having been already dispossessed of my property, I was least anxious to know anything more.

Without waiting for me, she resumed, "Today when I went to the market, I saw '*baba*' shivering with cold. He was running slight temperature also. I came back home, took some medicine and your gown. His physical need was certainly greater than your shameless material possession."

Here she paused for a few moments. Her natural smile had suddenly vanished. Some unusual seriousness was amply evident on her face. She looked at me. My eyes revealed eagerness to know more.

"And do you know what was he reading?"

Robbed by my own people, I was not interested in the hobbies and reading interests of others. I was like a helpless victim rendered lifeless by the undisputed authority of an autocrat. Still something in me wanted to know more about the old man.

"He was reading Gita...and...and it was in English."

I was completely floored by the words of my wife. 'His physical need was certainly greater than your shameless material possession...he was reading Gita...' These words kept on ringing in my ears, but I was more concerned with my loss.

Though there were no apparent reasons, I was little restless throughout the night. Mentally disturbed, I kept on rolling in my bed and could have a little wink of sleep only in the early morning hours. The office time also passed with some difficulty. In the evening, while returning from my office, I instinctively stopped near the old man. It was less for my gown and more for having a glimpse of the man who was unusually different from others.

I stood in front of the '*baba*'. He was not startled but looked up. He was a picture of serenity with a sublime radiance on his face. I looked at the gown, but did not want to ask him directly about the same. With a little hesitation, I touched his forehead and asked, "*Baba*, how are you feeling now?"

"Thank you very much, my son. I do not know whether I am better or worse but I do know that I am still living and enjoying the greatest gift of God."

"What can I do for you? Would you like to have some milk or tea?"

"No, thanks, my child. I would prefer to take nothing."

I wanted to stay there and was in search of some excuse. After a few moments of silence and having mustered a little more courage, I picked up Gita and said, "You appear to be a passionate reader of Gita."

"Yes. I have nothing else to do throughout the day. In distress, days are long and nights longer. Reading books, in fact, has always been my best pastime. This divine dialogue is my greatest source of inspiration." He took it from my hands and continued, "It contains not only deep philosophical concepts, but also the principles and techniques which, if put into practice, are extremely effective in unimaginable physical, mental and spiritual ways. This spiritual knowledge liberates us from the worldly bonds."

I was absolutely speechless to hear all this and could feel the throbbing of my heart. A little pause and he continued with an apparent sense of pride, "The Lord says, 'Abandon all duties, take refuge in Me alone. I shall liberate you from all sins, do no grieve.' One should completely surrender to His will and take shelter in His love."

The gown was now completely out of my mind and I was beginning to feel more comfortable in his company. Keen to know more, I continued, "What about your relatives? ...I mean your wife...your children and...and others."

Perhaps he was not prepared for such a sudden query. He evaded a specific reply. "Are you not my child? Are all those living here not my relatives?"

"Of course...but I mean..."

He reiterated his point. "This whole world is a big family and we are all children of the same God. Divine consciousness is present in every atom of the universe."

I was convinced that a specific reply to my question would not be forthcoming. Still I wanted to know more about him.

"You are right '*baba*'. All of us are children of the same God. I asked you about your family since I have always seen you sitting here all alone."

"Are you new to this place?"

"Yes, I have been transferred here only last month and do not know much about you. If you don't mind, please tell me something about you."

The '*baba*' paused for a few moments. He continued, "My life may be of little interest and value to you."

"Every life experience has something valuable to offer. Please tell me about your life," I pleaded.

"All people here know about me but since you have asked me, I don't want to disappoint you." A little pause and he continued, "Born in Montgomery, West Pakistan, I started my career as a school teacher after passing my matriculation. My only son started a small cloth business which prospered during the Second World War. My small happy family grew into a larger one and I had seven grand-daughters and one grand-son."

He paused for a moment and glanced at me to make sure that I was listening to him. Convinced of my keenness, he continued, "Those were the days of freedom struggle. Soon this struggle took the shape of mutual discord and gave rise to a grim succession of communal killings. There was panic everywhere and grave political conditions, supplemented by spiraling mob-violence, gripped the whole nation. Hatred needs a small trigger to turn violent. All social norms were broken with impunity and religious bigots set ablaze everything that came their way."

The dark shadows were beginning to lengthen. The evening temperature was falling. He looked at the setting sun. The earlier glow in his eyes was slowly fading and he appeared to be struggling to revive his memory. To help him gain confidence, I broke the silence and continued, "Yes, those were very tragic days and terror was rampaging everywhere. Everyone was living under the shadow of violence which had shaken the conscience of the nation. There was a turbulent wave of intolerance and unorganised anarchy flourished all around. Fanatics ignited communal passions everywhere. Chaos and misery reigned and people left their homes and hearths to take shelter in *gurudwaras* or in military camps. The innocent became an easy prey of the pent-up hostility of the reactionary forces and were the worst sufferers. We all became victims of this communal strife and hatred of man for man. Hatred can never be appeased by hatred. It can only be conquered by love and friendship."

"I vividly recall those days and the memory of the tragic events still haunts me. A horrendous tragedy hit my family. Curfew was clamped for days and when lifted for a few hours, my son went to the market to buy some essential commodities. On the way back, he was stabbed by a frenzied fanatic. He was bleeding profusely and there was no hope of his survival. The knife-wielding lunatics ran after him like hounds chasing a crippled hare. My son managed to come back home and locked the gate of the house. He lay on the floor in a critical condition and all of us were weeping and crying. The insane chasers shouted and tried to break open the gate. There was an imminent threat of death of all. The honour of the young girls was in grave danger. Fearing their brutality, and for the safety and chastity of his wife and young daughters, he implored us to immediately jump into the well which was in the courtyard of the house."

Unable to continue, he took a deep breath, cleared his parched throat and moistened his dry lips. With apparent agony and pain, he managed to continue, "We became victims of communal passion. We were under a grip of panic and an uncertain future. The whole family was plunged in grief. Death stalked straight in our eyes. All our wails and entities were in vain. With no ray of hope, all jumped into the well one by one. I was the last one to jump with my two-year-old grandson in my lap and am here to suffer the pain of my destiny."

He paused at regular intervals to gain the failing strength. I was horrified to hear the terrible tragedy. The *'baba'* was generally calm during all this narration and there was no appreciable change in his emotions. I had never heard of such a horrifying and hair-raising chilling tragedy. How could he suffer so much and live all these years with such a painful and heart-rending memory?

"Mysterious are the ways of God. We all wanted to die but providence had perhaps willed it otherwise. The blood-soaked hands of death snatched those who had to live. In a cruel twist of fate, one who had lived his age and should have been the first to die is still alive and sitting here before you."

There was a long pause. He looked at me and continued, "To complete the tragedy of my life, I miraculously survived being on top of the heap of lifeless bodies and some people took me out of the well after four days. Normalcy was restored and the city soon limped back to normalcy. There was no option but to flee the riot-torn city. After suffering untold hardships, I came to India with a caravan. There was none to share my grief and I finally came to terms with my tragedy. There was complete void and emptiness in my life except the homicidal memories. Loneliness is my only companion since then and I am trying to trace some solace in solitude."

"The blood-thirsty demons kill the innocent like a sport. How much you have suffered all these years? It is extremely tragic and painful to even imagine your harrowing tale of woes."

"All this is now a part of the painful past. We are all pawns on the chess-board of time whose movement is in invisible hands. I have no desire to live now."

"The whole world is in a grip of insanity. Why can't we live in peace and harmony? Why is the man enemy of man?" I provoked him to continue.

"Man by nature is greedy and selfish. Never-ending greed is the root cause of all our major social evils and mother of many crimes. It inspires violence. It gives birth to desires which arise like turbulent waves and we are easily swept away by them. It is like a bird that only flies in the sky and never comes to the ground. Desires are endless and even if fulfilled, our mind craves for more. They are insatiable as fire or as unquenched thirst. They are like an illusion or mirage and we are vainly running after them. Greed and desires create a stone wall between us and our happiness. Increasing desires decrease happiness and in mathematical terms, desires are inversely proportional to happiness. Problem is not in the abundance that we have, but in the little that others have. We are not grateful to God for what we have but pine for more and more. We must develop happiness as a way of thinking and doing."

After the much-needed little pause, he continued, "The world today is divided not only religiously but also nationally. Instead of living peacefully as human beings with love, with generosity, and without violence, we resort to hatred, brutality and antagonism. Also, one does not become spiritual by only visiting places of worship, following hollow dogmas, and performing outward sham rituals to please God. Ironically, silent prayers are louder and to please God is to love and respect His creation. Cleaning the mirror does not clean the image. We have to purify our inner self. We have locked our religions into separate air-tight fortresses, but God cannot be confined to these man-made structures. He is omnipresent. He is infinite and has neither beginning nor end. He is neither manifest nor non-manifest. He is formless. He is the ultimate. He is a mystery and is not conceivable. Just as sound of sea lies hidden in each sea shell, the vibration of God is hidden within every soul. This mysterious hidden vibration beacons us to tread the righteous path. To follow it or not is in our hands."

"It is unfortunate that we have become victims of hatred and violence. When will this hatred cease? Also, we have abandoned the path of spirituality."

He was deeply engrossed in some thought and waited for a while. Regained some strength and then continued, "Sun does not forget to shine on a poor man's hut. God bestows his blessings on everyone irrespective of caste, creed, religion or status. The quest for truth and knowledge is constant and will never end. Path of righteousness is the only road towards peace and tranquility. In our materialistic chase, we are abandoning this and are getting enchanted towards the worldly gains."

"The common man at times doesn't understand all this. What would you advise to people like us?"

"What advice can I give you? I am myself a learner and ignorant of the ultimate Truth. Still I would say, follow three super virtues: self-discipline, compassion and selflessness. Seek God within and in space around with the eyes of devotion to attain supreme eternal bliss and dwell in the spiritual realm. Follow the path of 'simple living and high thinking'. Surrender your false sense of ego and curtain of ignorance will be removed to enrich your life with continuous learning. Principle of universal brotherhood would eradicate all greed and communal discord. Humanity is one large single family. Remember, action is thy duty, reward is not thy concern. Proceed towards your goals with an even mind and divine help will come to you on its own."

"And to the children..."

"Children often come here and I enjoy their company most. They are as pure as God. I always tell them, dream big and keep on dreaming till they come true. Dreams are creators of a powerful energy. They lead to beliefs which, in turn, give rise to actions. Work hard to turn these dreams into reality. Give wings to your dreams and never let them sleep in your eyes. Banish all thoughts of defeat from your mind for only the strong shall inherit the earth. Do not despair in sorrow. Have faith in yourself and to dispel fear, face it. Seeds of determination lie deep within you and only they can fly who think they can. That is the secret of all the progress of mankind. The whole purpose is to enkindle self-confidence in the innocent minds."

"Your presence here is a source of great inspiration to all of us. I am sure people here will always remember you."

"When fresh flowers blossom on the trees, no one remembers even the colour of the earlier ones. I have now no desire to live," he continued as if making a prophecy.

"Please don't say this. We all pray for your long life."

"The ultimate has to come to everyone. But death is only a transformation where only the physical body perishes while the soul continues to exist. Death is simply separation of soul from the physical body and is the starting point of a new life. Life is a continuum. Life, death, pleasure, pain, joy and sorrow have no difference to me now and I have conquered the fear of death. I had ample share of all these in my life. I have nothing to lose now and so everything is a gain for me. Sorrow and pain were once my intimate companions but now I have overcome all of them. Time is passing. It will pass whether we like it or not and, come what may, the sun will rise again tomorrow. Life cannot stand still; it must go on like a caravan. I have now completely resigned myself to the will of God and am waiting for His call."

Feeling little exhausted, he evaded continuation and just murmured something not audible. Looking at his gown, he wrapped it firmly around his crouched body and suddenly switched over to another topic.

"A kind-hearted lady gave me this gown yesterday when I was shivering with cold and running temperature. She gave me some medicine also. I accepted all this, not because I desired this, but I did not want the giver to be disappointed. The pleasure of giving is more and I did not want to rob her of this sublime feeling."

I was momentarily reminded again of my gown but had no fascination for it now. I remained there for a few more moments to let his thoughts permeate deeper into my inner self. The '*baba*' had by now closed his eyes and was perhaps too weak to say anything more. Slowly, I made my way home pondering over the harsh and tragic realities of life. Drowned in the sea of thoughts, I reached home and took my dinner with a heavy heart. There was hardly any discussion at home. My wife had packed my clothes as next day I had to go out on an official tour.

I came back after a week. Immediately on my arrival, my son told me that the '*baba*' was no more. On the auspicious

Makar Sankranti day, he had joined other members of his family and had merged with the Light. People had collected some money for the last journey of the soul held in great reverence and my wife also contributed a bit. My son was one of the pal bearers and I was proud to hear this. The few moments spent with the *'baba'* had made a lasting impact on me and were significantly responsible for my inner transformation. They had completely transformed my conviction of life and the complexion of my thoughts. They had a profound influence on me and contributed immensely to a vital change in my philosophy of life. My approach and attitude to life had undergone a drastic change and my attachment with the materialistic world was beginning to diminish. The truth of ultimate reality had convinced me of the hollowness of man's greed and selfishness. My patched gown had given some warmth to one who had been deprived of the same by the ever-threatening fanatic devils of the society.

❐

2
A Leaf in the Garden

"Postman!"

Hearing the bell of the bicycle and the ever-welcome call of the postman, Babli, who was playing marbles in the courtyard of her house with her friends, immediately ran towards the door. The postman had already pushed inside a letter through a slit in the door.

"Babli, whose letter is that?" asked Charanjit from inside the kitchen. Without waiting for a reply, she peeped out, wiped drops of perspiration from her face with her '*dupatta*' and virtually ran towards her sister-in-law with her incongruously long plait swinging from side to side. She didn't want Babli to open the letter of her soul-mate.

"What are you doing, Babli?" shouted a visibly annoyed Charanjit and immediately snatched the letter from her.

"Why don't you allow me to open Veer's letter?"

Charanjit, a slim girl of elfin charm, affectionately patted the cheek of her innocent sister-in-law and did not care to answer knowing fully well that young Babli was too immature to understand such delicate issues. The letter had created ripples of joy in her heart and a glow of supreme ecstasy on her face as if she had achieved all that she had desired in her life. She dashed to the kitchen, lowered the flame of the stove, and started reading the letter. She was so engrossed in reading that she was completely unmindful of the fact that someone had quietly sneaked in unnoticed, managed to stand on a small wooden stool behind her and was trying to steal a few words from here and there.

"Why does Veer call you 'Channiji'?"

"You naughty girl! Will you go away from here?" She raised her hand and fained to hit Babli who immediately ran away, smiling and occasionally looking back.

Charanjit tried to catch hold of her tresses but the smart little girl quickly bent down and managed to slip away. She had always loved Babli who was about nine years old and was studying in class V. She had known her even before her marriage and, in fact, Babli was in one way instrumental in bringing Charanjit and Gurdeep emotionally closer to each other. This closeness had subsequently tied them in matrimonial knot.

Charanjit read the letter a number of times. She longed to read it over and over again, wishing the contents never to end. She glanced at every possible space where Gurdeep could have added a few words and made sure not to miss anything scribbled in the margins or corners.

The sweet words that Gurdeep was in the habit of writing had made Charanjit blush, kiss the letter and hide her face with it. He had advised her to look after her health and had given her some useful tips on child care. In the post script of the letter, which Charanjit had missed on first reading, Gurdeep wrote, "I have given your name as next of my kin. In case of any eventuality, you will be the first to receive information. You should not panic and must control yourself. Do not immediately disclose anything to Biji or to anyone else."

This forced a stream of tears suspended so far on the fringes of her eyes and the prophetic lines were all wet. The tears were relentlessly struggling to change the destiny of the writer. The luminous eyes had become dark and the delight of comely young lips had suddenly vanished.

Gurdeep had left Charanjit only one month after their marriage. The exigencies of duty had compelled him to leave when even the colour of henna had not faded on her hands. Letters, normally written once a week, were the only source of joy and romantic recollections. It was through these letters that a glorious future was being planned.

Not in the very distant past, Charanjit vividly remembered the day when she had joined the government school at Bhogpur, a small town on Jullundur-Pathankot railway line. She did not choose teaching. Teaching chose her and came to her as a matter of chance. Her father was initially reluctant to permit the mother-less child to go daily from Jullundur but yielded to the insistent pressure of his only child. Channi, as she was affectionately called by all, was the youngest member of the teaching faculty and could be easily mistaken as a school student. Soon she developed love for children and a liking for this noble profession.

Charanjit recalled the winter morning when a smart young man in military uniform entered the school premises, placed the kit-bag and iron suitcase at a distance and came to her when she was basking in the sun and supervising the children playing in the ground. After a moment's hesitation, the visitor looked at Charanjit and said, "Excuse me madam, my name is Gurdeep Singh. I want to meet Babli, I mean Balwinder Kaur. She is studying in class V. She is my sister." He said all this in one breath.

Charanjit was so fascinated by the smartness of the young man that she kept on looking at him and forgot to give a reply. Suddenly, she was interrupted by the teasing cough of a naughty fellow teacher standing close by.

"Channi, isn't Balwinder in your class?" asked the other teacher.

"Yes…yes, of course… Please wait for a moment. I will call Balwinder from my class."

"Thank you very much for the trouble, mam."

She left the playground and soon came back accompanied by a sweet little girl.

"Veerji!" the girl shouted from a distance and madly ran towards the young man who immediately hugged her and lifted her in his lap.

"How are you, Babli?"

Without caring to reply, Babli affectionately began to box her brother and asked, "Veer, why have you come after such a long time? I will not talk to you."

The young man embraced the loving child warmly and replied, "You know it was my training and leave is not permitted during this period. Moreover, taking leave is not easy in defence services."

"Then you better leave such a service and be a teacher in my school," replied Babli innocently.

The two teachers had a hearty laugh and Babli suddenly realised their presence. She immediately put her hands on her mouth and hid her face over the shoulder of her brother.

Charanjit was amazed at the spontaneous reply of the small child. She called her closer, hugged her affectionately, patted the blushed cheeks of the scared girl and said, "If everyone becomes a teacher, who will defend the borders and fight to save our motherland?"

Babli's age and innocence could not understand the deep philosophy behind Charanjit's query and even with her sharp wit and intellect was not in a situation to reply. She was fortunately rescued from any further embarrassment when another girl brought a glass of water.

"Please have some water. You may be feeling thirsty," said Charanjit while offering the glass of water to Gurdeep.

"Yes, indeed I am. Thank you very much."

Having quenched his thirst, Gurdeep requested permission for taking Babli home. Charanjit nodded her head in affirmation and turning towards Babli said, "Babli, go and bring your bag."

Babli was virtually mad with joy. She ran to her classroom and immediately brought her bag. In excitement and ecstasy, Babli had forgotten to zip her bag and pencils, lunch-box and other things started falling out of the bag. She was looking back and telling her friends at the top of her voice, "I am going home. My Veer has come."

"Look Babli! You are dropping things all over the place." said Charanjit.

She immediately handed over the bag to her brother and ran back to pick up the fallen articles. She was about to go with Gurdeep when the disciplined soldier asked her to seek permission from her teacher.

"May I go, madam?"

"Yes, you may go," replied Charanjit with a smile.

"Thank you, madam," replied Babli.

"Babli, don't forget to bring some sweets for us tomorrow," said the other teacher while Gurdeep and Babli turned their back. Gurdeep glanced over his shoulder and, in his heart of hearts thanked Charanjit with a loving smile.

In the very first meeting, seeds of mutual love were sown and both developed a strong innate attraction for each other. Gurdeep was fascinated by the sweet smile and charming looks of Charanjit. Impelled by a latent urge, he decided to steal momentary glimpses of the teacher everyday on the railway station at the time of the opening and closing of the school. Stolen glances thus exchanged began to convey more than words and love began to blossom silently but rapidly. Charanjit on her part was also irresistibly drawn closer to his dream-guy and was equally impatient to see him everyday. Babli became the convenient medium of information for both and the innocent girl failed to understand the sudden spurt in the emotional behaviour of both. On the pretext of knowing about her progress in studies, Gurdeep also paid a few formal visits to the school. The last such meeting on the day of Gurdeep's departure was rather sad and painful for both.

After a few moments of hesitation, Gurdeep broke silence and said, "Thank you for all the trouble that I gave to you all these days."

"Please don't say that. It was my duty," replied Charanjit with a lump in her throat.

"I request you to look after Babli…She is the only hope of our family…" Gurdeep's voice was suddenly choked and he could not complete the sentence.

"You need not worry about her education. I will pay personal attention to her so long as I am here."

"Why, are you going somewhere else?"

"No. Not so soon. I am working on a leave vacancy and shall be relieved as soon as the regular teacher joins. Still I hope to be here for about six more months."

"It is rather sad. I pray for your stay here."

"Man is a slave of time and destiny determines the course of our lives. Even if I wish to stay here, providence may will it otherwise."

A few moments of silence and Gurdeep resumed, "Babli is now under your care. Please look after her and keep my mother informed about her progress even if you have to specially go to her. I am leaving today. My leave is over."

"Days have passed so quickly…Hope we shall meet soon," said Charanjit rather hesitatingly.

"To meet and depart is the way of life but to depart and meet again is the hope of life." Gurdeep sounded very philosophical in his reply.

Charanjit just looked at him, blushed and lowered her eyes. Gurdeep had come to the school with the intention of talking quite a lot but failed to muster enough courage. The strength of the young soldier was drowned in the sea of love. Both took recourse to silence to express their latent feelings of love. Gurdeep finally got up, folded his hands, reluctantly turned back and left the school. Charanjit also could not say anything and folded her hands in reply.

A week later, Charanjit received a letter for the first time from someone at her school address. She could not recognise the handwriting. Some strange inner feeling predicted it to be from Gurdeep, though reason was unable to explain this feeling. With a sweet sensation in her heart, she opened the letter with trembling hands. She was completely amazed. Her prediction was correct. It was indeed a letter from Gurdeep.

"Dear Charanjit,

I could not say all that I wanted to say at the time of my departure. Babli is actually not my sister. She is the daughter of my elder sister. My sister died only four days after her birth and her father was killed in a family feud. Since then, she has stayed with us and has been brought up by my mother. She is, however, unaware of all these facts and we do not want her to know till she is grown up and mature enough to understand all this. She is the hope of our ruined life and I am sure you will look after her. This is my personal request, though perhaps I have no right to give you this trouble. I do not know why I am writing all this to you…" In a corner, he had scribbled, "Hope to see you soon."

There was nothing unusual in the letter but she was excited to meet Gurdeep soon. She immediately called Babli, embraced her and showered all the love on her. Babli was completely amazed at the sudden change in the behaviour of her teacher. Little did she realise that it was through her that love was being transferred to someone else. Charanjit had already started liking Babli and the bonds of love and affection with the little orphan girl had been further strengthened with the receipt of this letter. She was now a regular visitor to Gurdeep's house and had become a darling of his mother too.

Gurdeep had requested for a reply and this paved the way for an endless chain of letters. Though Babli was the focus of prime attention in these letters, they brought Gurdeep and Charanjit emotionally closer to each other and each longed to meet the other at the earliest opportunity. Undaunted by the rumors of her love affairs and damaging gossips of colleagues, the exchange of letters continued unaffected.

Gurdeep was about to come for his annual leave and Babli was too anxious to reveal this news to her teacher. She was unaware that her teacher had already received the information from Gurdeep.

"Madam, my Veer is coming home next Monday."

"Is it?"

"Yes. I will bring him to school when he comes."

"Please do that," requested Charanjit. Drawing her closer to her body, she hugged her tightly and asked, "What will your Veer bring for you?"

"He will bring new suits for me and for Biji."

"And what will you give me?" teased Charanjit.

"I will give you one suit out of that," promised the little girl.

Charanjit could not help planting a sweet affectionate kiss on her rosy cheek. Babli instantly came closest to her teacher and said, "I am sorry madam, I forgot to tell you. Biji has called you at home today."

During the few occasional visits, Gurdeep's mother had developed great liking for Charanjit. She was fascinated by her childlike smile, charming looks and caring nature.

"Babli, your Charanjit teacher is very affectionate. I like her very much."

"Yes Biji, she loves me too. In fact, all students like her very much."

"Should we request her to permanently stay in our home?"

Babli screamed with joy and immediately clung to her grandmother. Putting her tiny hands around her neck, she replied, "Yes Biji, let her stay here forever. She will help me in my studies too."

The old woman just smiled, for her innocent grand-daughter was too young to comprehend her real latent intentions.

On the day of Gurdeep's arrival, his dream-girl received him at Jullundur railway station. Dressed in light blue *kameez-salwar* with matching *dupatta* and crimson rose-bud decoratively tucked in her braid, she was looking stunningly beautiful. Overwhelmed with joy, she accompanied him to Bhogpur. On reaching Bhogpur, Gurdeep was surprised to see his mother and Babli at the railway station. Realising that his mother had seen Charanjit with him, he immediately touched her feet and said, "Biji, she is Charanjit…I mean Charanjit Kaur…She is Babli's teacher."

The mother looked at her son, managed a faint smile and embraced Charanjit. "Come Channi, come with us."

"I will come later on, Biji. I have to go to the school."

Gurdeep was completely stunned. How did his mother know about Charanjit's nickname? She had met her as if she had known her very intimately.

At dinner, Gurdeep was keen to narrate an incident about one of his colleagues but his mother was least interested. Shifting the focus of discussion, she said, "Gurdeep, now that you have completed your training, I am not prepared to listen to your lame excuses. I want to find a suitable match and marry you during your leave."

"But where is the hurry, Biji?"

"It may not be for you but I want to see my grandson before I close my eyes."

"For you Biji, I am prepared to do everything," replied the obedient son.

"I have already selected a girl for you."

Gurdeep was surprised and was completely speechless. He looked at his mother with searching eyes.

"What is your idea about Channi?" The old lady suddenly threw a pleasant surprise.

"Channi! Who is she?"

"Now don't be innocent. You can't fool me. After all, I am your mother."

Babli, who was sitting at a distance and engrossed in doing her home-work, immediately rushed to her grandmother and said, "Biji, my teacher is very good. I also like her very much. Please arrange Veer's marriage with her."

"Charanjit's father is also very keen about this alliance," continued Biji.

"But Biji, how do you know her father?" enquired Gurdeep.

"After your last departure, Charanjit often came to our home. She loved Babli very much. I also developed a liking for her and wished her to be a part of our family. One of my cousins has joined the sugar mill here and one day I went to meet him. Babli was with me and by chance, Channi and her father, who are distantly related to my cousin, had also come to meet him. It was there that Charanjit's father opened the topic of her daughter's marriage and I agreed to make Charanjit my daughter-in-law."

"Has Charanjit accepted the proposal?"

"Don't worry about her. You tell me your decision."

"What can I say? If you have already decided, I can't say anything." Flashing a shy smile, Gurdeep replied hesitatingly, though inwardly he was happy for Channi was his heart-throb.

Babli was so excited and overwhelmed with joy that she immediately ran to the kitchen to bring some sweets for all to celebrate the happy decision. She also took no time to announce this marriage proposal to her friends in the school. Taking advantage of Gurdeep's leave, the marriage was arranged in a fortnight. The days of happy married life began to pass very quickly.

In the evening, they would often go out of the town, holding hands and reveling in each other's company. Physical urge would draw them further closer to each other and for hours, they would be engrossed in romantic discussions enjoying the breath-taking beauty of moon and stars. One night, while treading the winding paths of the fields on a full moon breezy night, Gurdeep revealed, "I have two desires in my life. I wish to have a small garden on the outskirts of Bhogpur where beautiful flowers may grow and where small children may merrily play, radiating their love and message of peace all around."

"I could never imagine that a soldier could have such a soft heart for children and be a lover of the beauty of nature. Well, may I know the other wish?" asked Charanjit.

"Life should be big, may not be long and, as a soldier, I should face the bullet on my chest and not on my back," was the prompt reply.

"For God's sake, please don't talk about these things. You want me to weep?"

"All right, I will talk about something else," said Gurdeep bringing her closer to him. "Do you know I have received a telegram today?"

"No, I don't know."

"I have been recalled by my regiment. My leave has been cancelled."

Charanjit was extremely sad to hear this. She had been reading in the newspapers about the mounting tension brewing on the borders and feared the war clouds hovering over the sky.

"Tell me how I shall pass my days?" said Charanjit while forcing her tears to remain hidden in her eyes.

"Forget about all this. Let us enjoy the moment." Gurdeep could understand her feelings and tried to change her mood. He broke the seriousness of the situation and said, "I shall try to take some leave and come back soon."

"All these are hollow consolations."

Gurdeep left next morning, leaving Charanjit to bear silently the pangs of separation. Though outwardly calm and composed, she was inwardly sad and dejected. Having married a soldier, she had to prepare herself for all these eventualities and ups and downs in her married life. Letters again became the medium of joy, happiness and consolation in the trying times.

Shy by nature, Charanjit would normally read Gurdeep's letters in privacy even though there was no need of any secrecy now. While reading the letters in the kitchen, the whole sequence of romantic days of the past would flash before her eyes just in the space of few moments. On one such occasion, she was unaware of the arrival of her mother-in-law while she was deeply engrossed in her sweet dreams. A warm hand on her shoulder suddenly brought her back to the realms of reality.

"Channi, my child, what is the matter?"

"Nothing. Nothing, Biji," replied Charanjit with trembling lips. She quickly wiped the dried tears and forced a semblance of joy on her face.

"What has Gurdeep written?"

"His regiment has moved to an unknown place and he may not be very regular in writing letters."

"Don't worry, my child. I am here with you. I will look after you properly. In these days, you should not have any tension in your mind for this may affect the health of the baby."

"I am not thinking of this, Biji," replied Charanjit with an apparent sense of confidence and continued, "I am thinking of wars. Why do they break out? Isn't it a curse that brother is slitting the throat of brother? Why can't we all live in peace?"

"My child, wars have been waged in the past and shall continue in future also...You should not worry about all these things. You should do your duty as a mother. Come, let us have lunch now. I am feeling very hungry," consoled the mother-in-law. With all the heaviness in her heart, she could not continue the discussion any further.

Charanjit was sent to Jullundur for her first delivery, medical facilities being better there. She gave birth to a daughter and wanted Gurdeep to be informed immediately. Surprisingly, instead of the expected jubilations, there was an atmosphere of hushed silence all around. All those, who came to see her, sat there for a few moments, whispered a few words and left without even having a glimpse of the new-born child. It looked as if a pal of gloom had engulfed the whole house and there was a state of mourning all around.

Normally, the birth of the first child should have brought a wave of happiness and rejoicing in the family. Instead, there was sadness on all faces and silence on all lips. Charanjit was utterly confused and had spasms of fear and doubt in her mind. She attributed all this to the birth of a daughter, birth of a son being more welcome in her society. Her mother-in-law had arrived a few days before the delivery and though quite happy in the beginning, was suddenly serious after the birth of the child. Babli was the only exception who was full of excitement and was not prepared to leave the baby even for a moment.

Charanjit was keen to know the cause of the distressing atmosphere and said, “Biji, I know you are sad for you wanted to have a grandson. I have not fulfilled your wish.”

“Channi, my child…” She hugged her and the little child and burst into tears.

Some inner feeling made Charanjit more suspicious. “Biji, why are you weeping like that? What is the matter? Is everything all right?”

Channi’s father, who was standing close by, turned his face away and also started weeping. The truth could not be concealed any longer. On Charanjit’s insistence to know the reason, he placed a telegram before his daughter to break the most unfortunate news. The telegram had been received a few hours before the birth of the child. It was addressed to

Charanjit Kaur but was received and opened by her father. He did not reveal the contents at that moment of tension. Gurdeep was no more. He had died a martyr's death. Even in the wildest of her imaginations, Charanjit could never dream of this to be the cause of the prevailing gloomy silence. It was as if a mountain of sorrows had fallen on her. Her whole body was pale and lifeless like a statue. Holding the baby tight against her breast, she began to cry violently. All efforts to console her proved futile. Unable to bear the shock, she became unconscious.

Time plays strange games and life changes hues every moment. Two days after the birth of the child, Charanjit received a letter from Gurdeep. For a moment, she thought, maybe the telegram was false. Maybe Gurdeep was alive. Some divine intervention may have saved him. With these mixed feelings of distress and hope, she opened the letter. Her hands were trembling. Normally very long, this one was very short. The letter had been written by Gurdeep a day before his death and it was as if he had made a prophecy. "You never know your fate in war. I am not a coward, but if anything goes wrong, look after Biji and Babli. I know that we shall have a daughter. Name her Rani. Bring her up properly and educate her." In the post script, he wrote, "I do not want you to be sad in life. Never weep. Whenever alone, peep into your heart. I will be there."

What an irony of fate? Happiness and sorrow always played hide-and-seek with Charanjit. Happiness came to her intermittently and in small doses. Periods of joy were shorter and those of pain were longer. Years of agony and not moments of happiness were in store for her. Happiness had gone miles away and she had grown too weak to chase it. Deprived of the love of a mother in childhood, her father provided her with all the needed comforts and made her forget the loss of a mother. Her mother-in-law filled the void created by her mother and treated her as her own daughter. Gurdeep came in her life like a short sweet dream, only to be shattered soon by the cruel hands of destiny. His loss had created a complete void in her life. After him, the old lady was a pillar of great strength and provided immense emotional support to her. She always tried to ease the pain of Charanjit's loneliness and once even placed the proposal of her re-marriage. Charanjit refused it point blank as she always wanted to live and die as Gurdeep's wife. Even the last hope of happiness was soon destined to be shadowed by thick clouds of gloom. The old lady was soon completely broken from within and was unable to bear the tragic loss of her young son. She died a peaceful death and did not get up from sleep one morning. Unexpected and untimely death of this loved one was another colossal loss for Charanjit.

Even the darkest night has prospects of a bright morning but no dawn lay ahead in Charanjit's long and painful widowed life. Death is a tragedy not for the dead but for the living. Her tiny dreamland was completely shattered into fragments and the realms of gloom knew no bounds. Life had come to a standstill and appeared to be only an illusion. She had no option but to face its trials and tribulations with determination. She was prepared to fight the grim battle of loneliness and face the succession of challenges with courage, for Gurdeep had desired her not to shed tears. Happiness had betrayed her and she was restrained from sharing her sorrows with others. Coupled with all these sorrows was the financial strain and burden of bringing up a small family of young Babli and Rani. Her self-respect did not permit her to turn to her father for help and she decided to spend the remainder of her life at Bhogpur.

The nation soon recognised the bravery of Gurdeep and he was awarded Param Vir Chakra posthumously on the Republic Day. Charanjit was invited to receive the same. On this sad, depressing and somber occasion, she completely forgot all the sorrows for a moment. Clad in milk-white *kameez-salwar* and *shawl,* she proudly climbed the steps to receive the prestigious gallantry award. "...He displayed most conspicuous and exemplary courage in the face of grave adversities and faced bullets on his chest to save the besieged soldiers..."

Charanjit came home with the award. She placed the medal before the photograph of Gurdeep and began to cry. The tears lightened her heart but failed to lessen the pain of the tragic loss. Gurdeep's home-town was also proud of his sacrifices. Soon money was collected to erect a statue in the memory of the deceased soldier. Land for this had been donated by the authorities on the outskirts of Bhogpur.

The moments of pride, as usual with us, were soon forgotten and the pain of abject poverty, misery and desperation began to weigh heavily on the unfortunate family. Charanjit's repeated requests and frantic efforts fortunately bore fruit and she was appointed a primary teacher on compassionate grounds. The life became busy and began to pass more smoothly. She devoted herself whole-heartedly to her school duties and the education of the two unfortunate girls. Whatever time was left was devoted to silent worship, cleaning the *Gurudwara* premises, serving the devotees, and helping the people in distress. The teachings of the Gurus were cultivating her inner strength. She was convinced that destiny plays a vital role in our lives and some unseen power manoeuvres all our moves. All that happens is so ordained and is for the good of all.

With her little savings from the meager salary, she developed Gurdeep's memorial into a beautiful rose garden and a playground for children. In the beginning, there was substantial gathering every year on Martyr's Day to commemorate the sacrifice of Gurdeep and other martyrs. With the passage of time, there used to be very modest crowd including Charanjit, Babli and Rani. The memory of supreme sacrifices soon faded and people forgot about those who sacrificed love and comfort of their children so that others may enjoy and live in peace. After all, soldiers and God are remembered in days of misery, only to be forgotten in times of peace. She knew that sun shines, rivers flow, birds sing and trees bear fruit without any acknowledgement. She too had no expectations now.

Time lessens agony and heals painful wounds caused by the loss of dear ones. But wounds of Charanjit were as fresh today as ever. Babli and Rani had grown up. Babli was married and settled in the States. She had arranged a suitable match for her niece there and Rani was soon to leave her mother, alone and sojourn. With a heavy heart, she agreed to the proposal as she realised that birds lose their strength by remaining on the ground. The grief-stricken mother was happy at the future prospects of her daughter and for having fulfilled Gurdeep's dream. Distance from both Babli and Rani was disturbing but despite repeated imploring from all, she decided to face and fight the circumstances and remained attached to her culture and traditions in India.

She voluntarily chose life of isolation and did not mingle much with the people. Haunted by loneliness and feeling of despair and dejection, she had now learnt to suffer in silence and seek solace in the happiness of others. She had torn off the soiled pages from the book of her life and had completely resigned herself to the will of God. Time had stagnated in distress. Tears were by now completely dried in the dark sunken eyes and the charming flower had withered even before it had fully blossomed. Happiness had gone miles away and she was now too weak to chase it. Youth had completely faded under the burden of sorrows and her well-groomed grey hair was now normally tied in a bun. Light wrinkles on her face were discernable but she still retained her youthful glow on her face.

Money was not a problem but it could not fill the permanent void in her life. She had come to terms with her losses and was facing the upheavals of life with composure. She had refused to be dragged down by sufferings and was determined to face life with courage as there could be no retake or 'U'-turn in the road of her life. She would often smile herself and treasure the memory of the past golden moments. Evergreen love of the past had transformed her pain into occasional pleasure. She was now like a deserted dry leaf on the ground that once adorned a beautiful tree in the garden, broken by the cruel hands of destiny and brought to the ground spiraling and floating. Puppet in His hands, He gives with both hands and can leave us like a dry leaf unmindful of the place where it would fall on the ground. Having no strength of its own, the unseen forces of wind and storm were now mercilessly blowing it from one corner to the other, leaving it completely to the mercy of time and nature.

After the school time, she was often seen in her milky-white *salwar, kameez* and *dupatta* sitting on the platform of the statue of her husband lost in thought about the day when man would conquer hatred, mistrust and prejudice and live with tolerance and understanding. In the darkness of the past, she was searching for dawn of future. Lonely in the crowded world and none to share her sorrows, she was struggling to live the present, forget the past and find some solace in appreciating the inexplicable beauty of nature, loved so much by Gurdeep. In nature, she would visualise a glimpse of God and closeness to the Divine. She would often catch the fiery orb of the sun sinking low behind the flowering trees and think of the dawn of the morrow. At night, she would often look at the moon where Gurdeep's face would be visible to her in its contours. In her spirit of optimism, she would often say:

Grieve not, complain not,
All will be well.
Dark clouds will wither one day,
Bright sunshine will come.
Have faith in Him,
He will bless as He has done."

The spectacular sight that she loved most and witnessed for hours was of the giggles of small children flocking the garden in the evening, laughing and playing their innocent games. In her quest for the final peace, she would keenly watch chirping sparrows sitting on soft petals and enjoying the nectar of flowers. Happiness sometimes flashed through some hidden corners and she longed to be a part of the flock of birds flying in unison striving to go back to their nests in the evening to join their families. All her sorrows were drowned in the sight of the blue sky, floating clouds, blooming flowers and in the rhythm of the rustling leaves. In this perfect balance of Nature, she discovered a soothing solace and never gave in to loneliness. She had now learnt to rejoice in the present.

Charanjit knew that the departed never come back again and only leave their memories behind. Still a voice from within bid her that Gurdeep would come back one day to take her Channi to join him in eternal peace in the celestial abode. Lonely in life, she did not want to be lonely in death. Sitting on the platform of Gurdeep's statue, she would hear the distant echo and wait patiently for the arrival of that moment.

❐

3
A Log of Wood

'Masterji', as he was respectfully addressed, occupied a place of great reverence, honour and dignity in rural culture and was always greeted with folded hands by young and old alike. People held him in high esteem and invariably offered him a higher seat. He became a symbol of veneration since the day he landed in that small village, located amid sandy deserts infested with snakes. The nearest city was thirty kilometres away. The nearest road was about three kilometres from the village and one kilometre from the school. The bus used to come from the city three times a day and the common modes of transport were bicycle and camel-cart.

Masterji joined the high school here as a teacher of science and mathematics. He was a handsome young man of just twenty. Frail in body, he was soft-spoken and normally very well-dressed. Born and brought up in an urban society, he was completely unfamiliar with rural culture. By virtue of his good nature and devotion to duty, he made a deep impact on students and his name soon became a household word. Young girls and married women often passed by the side of the school to fetch water from the village-well or on their way to the fields. The normal make-up of the married women was the thick stem of vermilion powder in the centre parting of their hair, a decorative *'tika'* on the forehead and heavy silver ornaments in arms, neck and legs. Their normal attire consisted of long scarf which covered their head and face, a blouse and long skirt. They were all muti-coloured and decorated with beads and small mirrors that reflected light. Dress of unmarried girls was the same except that it was not so decorative and the colours were less bright. With a row of three to four earthen or metal pitchers balancing on their heads, they would stealthily try to glance through their veils to have a momentary glimpse of the smart teacher. The looks of the young girls on the same routine were also invariably glued towards him and their teasing laugh would at times embarrass the shy young teacher. The amount of respect that he was going to command became evident on a night only about a month after his joining the school.

On that fateful early-monsoon night, Masterji decided to sleep in the verandah of the school. The night was pitch-dark and the sky was overcast with threatening clouds that had started gathering since evening. All alone in the large school building, the chicken-hearted teacher was virtually trembling with fear and loneliness. He was terribly afraid of sleeping in his make-shift bedroom, created by partitioning the science laboratory with the help of almirahs. That evening, a young woman had been cremated in the cremation ground that shared a common boundary with the school. The window of the science laboratory was barely twenty metres from the smouldering remains of the cremated body. The woman had died an unnatural death and it was a common belief among the villagers that the ghost of the woman would wander at night. The school sweeper-cum-watchman had been recently married and the kind-hearted Masterji often allowed him to stay at home at night. Loneliness, thunder, lightening, fear of the ghost and rustling of leaves due to the strong wind had all added to his state of fear. Added to this was the fear of frequently crawling snakes in the sandy area around the school. To ward off the mortal fear, he kept himself busy by invoking goddess *Durga* and mumbling '*Hanuman Chalisa*' under the breath.

All these frightening experiences were unusual for the soft-spoken teacher who had just come out of a protected home life. He inwardly cursed the day he landed there and decided to stay in the school building. The villagers, with all the respect that they bestowed on him as a '*guru*' of their children, were indeed very conservative and not prepared to give on rent even a small room for his stay in their houses. The houses were also such that sparing a room would have certainly disturbed their privacy, the women observing complete '*purdah*' from the elders and strangers of all ages.

Masterji had hardly managed to sleep on that dreadful night when he was suddenly awakened by the exuberant laughter of some people. He was dead scared and fear prompted him to cover his face immediately with the bed-sheet. His act was more like the pigeon that closes his eyes on seeing a cat, believing that the cat is also not looking at him.

"Hey! Who is sleeping there?"

A loud resonant voice echoed in his ears. He was too terrified to respond or peep out of the covering. The yell was repeated and Masterji was now convinced that it was not a dream or a ghost. Unable to avoid a reply, the terrified teacher poked his head out of the bed sheet, wiped the drops of perspiration from his face and stammered, "I…I am a teacher …a teacher of this school."

"Oh *guruji*! We are sorry to disturb you. Please enjoy your sleep. We just wanted to have a *'lota'* to drink some water from the well."

One person out of the three took the *'lota'* lying on a stool near the bed and went towards the well, just about twenty metres away. The awe-struck Masterji heard some heated discussion among the three. He could not make head or tail of the same, mainly because of his unfamiliarity with the local dialect. Each pulsating moment appeared to be longer than an hour but fortunately for him, the time passed peacefully. The three strangers departed and there was again complete silence after their departure. The poor teacher was just preparing to lie down when one of the strangers, who appeared to be heavily drunk and was struggling to stand on his legs, appeared again. He bowed down and said with folded hands, "Masterji, we are sorry to disturb you in your sleep." Keeping in his lap a small bundle that he was carrying, he resumed, "*Guruji,* I was very keen to meet you. My son is studying in your school in class V and he always praises you. Let me confess, I am a very bad character and don't want my son to follow in my footsteps. I want to educate him and wish him to be a good human being. I request you with folded hands to look after him. Please don't mind if I come and meet you today evening." He tried to touch his feet, which the frightened teacher dragged away because of fear and embarrassment.

The stranger became emotional. His voice was chocked. Unable to continue further, he got up, silently folded his hands again and left. Masterji was completely amazed and surprised at the behaviour of the stranger. Who was he? Why was he keen to meet him? How could his son be protected from the baneful and unhealthy influence of the father?

Drowned in these thoughts, he could have a wink of sleep only towards the dawn and was awakened by the sweet voice of Jhabar Singh, the sweeper-cum-watchman, who entered the school premises singing his self-composed '*ragni*'. In one breath, Masterji immediately narrated to him the complete details of the harrowing episode.

"Masterji, it happens here sometimes. The strangers who came here at night were actually thieves. After some heroic plunder, they must have been fighting over the sharing of the booty which you could not comprehend. The person who stayed back and talked to you, I am sure, was Hari Singh, a very shady character of this area. He is more commonly known as 'Haria *Pehlwan*'. Wrestling was his profession but he abandoned it at the prime of his youth and fell a prey to the world of crime. For some time, he was persuaded by his wife to give up the path of crime and lead an honest life, but you know Masterji, crime follows a criminal like a shadow and the two cannot be separated. Habits can change; not the nature. His son, only ten years old, is a champion camel rider of this area and all believe that he will leave his father far behind in his profession. Masterji, I am a completely illiterate person but I will suggest that you avoid meeting him. Enmity and friendship of such people are both dangerous and may tarnish your good image. You are new to this place and are a thorough gentleman. Kindly keep yourself away from the dirty local politics. I also request you not to talk to anyone about this incident. Though police will not come here for any enquiry, it is better to pose ignorance about the incident." After a little pause, he continued, "But sir, there is nothing to worry and nobody will harm you. People here have great respect and reverence for the teachers."

The incident had two deep impacts on Masterji. Criminals everywhere have identical motives but appear to distinctly differ in their attitude in rural and urban culture. In big cities, they have no respect for anyone and mercilessly rob the people, even in broad day-light, irrespective of their age, sex or profession. He could hardly believe that in rural culture, they would be so respectful to a teacher and so deeply concerned about the future of their children. He also appreciated the sincere and sound advice of the completely illiterate watchman and realised that wisdom was not the monopoly of the literate only. He was now getting inwardly convinced that his stay in that remote village, three hundred kilometres from his hometown, would be quite safe.

Next day was Sunday. In the afternoon, the watchman came running to Masterji while he was busy in his studies. He was completely out of breath. While tucking his shabby and patched '*dhoti*' and squatting on the floor by the side of the chair, he said, "Masterji, Haria *Pehlwan*, one who talked to you last night, has murdered a man. It is said that his comrades in crime doubted his integrity and suspected him to have cheated them. One of them came to his house today to settle the score. Both had heated discussion over the value of the booty. Haria, it is said, argued that the target was spotted by him and he deserved a lion's share while others discounted his reasoning. According to them, all were equal partners in the catch. The situation soon turned explosive and the visitor threatened Hari Singh with dire consequences. He suddenly whipped out his dagger and pounced upon Haria. Seeing that her husband was in danger, his wife took the axe lying there and in one stroke, chopped off the head of the attacker. People say that to save his wife, Haria *Pehlwan* has claimed responsibility of the gruesome murder. The actual reality and details are not known. Men, women and children have flocked his house to have a glimpse of the *Pehlwan* and his wife. Strong police contingent has arrived and his house is turned into a garrison. I came here to inform you and am going back to gather further details."

"It is really shocking to hear this tragic episode but all those who embrace the world of crime, rot in jail. His confessional statement may save him from the gallows but will result in at least life imprisonment."

"It is a common saying in our area that as you sow, so shall you reap. If you spread thorns, you can't gather flowers. Haria had to pay for his crimes one day," saying this, the watchman immediately departed.

Every cloud has a silver lining. Though the tragic incident made Masterji sad, he felt relieved that the meeting with Hari Singh was naturally out of question now. He began to ponder over the mental and physical strength of the women-folk. Men were generally busy in smoking, drinking and playing cards while women worked hard both at home and in the fields. This had made them physically even stronger than men.

Masterji's personal difficulties began to worry him more than the fate of Hari Singh or his family. The basic problems of boarding and lodging had been taking away most of his time and he was unable to concentrate on his studies. Though the problem of accommodation was immediately and conveniently solved by bending the rules and occupying part of the school building, cooking meals remained completely unsolved. For miles together, there was not even a small '*dhaba*'. A store-room of the school near its gate had been converted into a kitchen by Shankar Dayal Sharma, the waterman of the school. Students respectfully called him 'Panditji'. He was in his late forties, with grey hair but eyes always lighting up with a twinkle. He was a very jovial character, a radio of local news and was never short of rumours. Helpful by nature, he was an excellent cook and came to the rescue of the teachers who decided to stay there temporarily. This arrangement was convenient for the teachers and would also provide some additional income to his large family, a complete football team of children. He was still going strong and was soon expecting the 'twelfth man' of his team.

The members of the kitchen increased from one to five, a teacher and three students also deciding to stay in the school campus. The students belonged to a little far off village and stay in the school gave them enough time to study and also seek the necessary guidance from the ever-willing Masterji. Charan Singh, the new teacher, came on transfer and his village was about one hundred kilometres away. 'Chaudharyji, as he was popularly addressed, was a burly wrestler in his mid-forties and his appearance evoked awe and fear at first sight. By nature, he was a thorough gentleman and a very kind-hearted person. He was an extremely buoyant character and a store-house of rustic jokes. He was always ready with an appropriate one for every occasion which would send all into peals of laughter.

The two teachers had more differences than similarities. Their social backgrounds were diametrically opposite and age separated them by a generation. Their hobbies and habits were poles apart. One had reckless appetite and would normally take over two dozen '*chapaties*', the other was a poor eater of not more than three '*chapaties*'. One was chirpy and hilarious while the other was shy, reserved and a lover of silence. One had a heart of steel, the other of a chicken. One spent his spare time in sleeping and smoking *hookah*, the other was wedded to books. One felt he had achieved all in life, the other had hardly made a beginning. Similarities, though few, were significant. Both were very faithful to their profession and sincere to their duties. Their basic philosophy on the corrupt social system and sinking human values was identical. Because of these similarities both soon became close friends. Chaudhary's presence was a boon to the inexperienced and innocent Masterji and shielded him from the baneful effects of local politics. In course of time, he became a pillar of strength for the young teacher in motivating him for a bright future.

Chaudhary was a fit choice to be the in-charge of the school hostel. Not burdened with heavy teaching duties, he could afford lot of spare time and solve the problems of the kitchen. He looked after the purchases properly and the arrangements became more smooth and regular. His keen observant eye, however, could not check the Pandit from making some market penny, who would still save something to buy tobacco for the '*hookah*' which he would normally share with the Chaudhary. With better management, the quality of food improved considerably, though it continued to be spicy with lot of fat.

All necessities for the hostel could be purchased from the farmers or the village '*bania*' but the firewood was a perpetual problem, for it was scarce in and around the village. Cooking-gas was hardly known even in big cities in those days and kerosene oil was available only for lighting purpose. The village-women were in the habit of using cow-dung cakes which could not be used in the school kitchen on account of the non-availability of the material and the labour involved in the process. Transporting coal from the nearest city was not economically viable. Wood was the only solution which could be purchased when some tree was cut.

The other alternative which was more common was to collect twigs from the jungle which Pandit was kind enough to do. Where such essential commodities were a grave problem, luxuries of urban life were only a distant dream.

With the advent of the rainy season, Pandit pressed the panic button and raised a banner of revolt. He was fuming with anger when he entered the school premises. He adjusted his white turban and went straight to Chaudhary. Throwing an ultimatum, he said, "Chaudhary Sahib, I am not going to collect the firewood for you from the jungle. The rains are about to set in. You better purchase some dry wood and store it for the kitchen." Chaudhary was quite a shrewd character and he immediately understood that Pandit was in a terrible mood and reaction in anger would create another problem rather than solving one. It was essential to soften Pandit's temper. He smiled, closed his nostrils with his fingers and then strongly breathed in, as was his normal habit and said, "Once it so happened, Panditji, that a very strong and invincible wrestler was defeated in a bout. Instead of taking the defeat in a sporting way, he was extremely furious. He came home and immediately started beating his wife with a stick while she was kneading the flour for preparing '*chapaties*' for the dinner. Hearing her loud cries, the neighbours gathered and enquired about the cause.

"This lady has made my life miserable. She doesn't know how to behave," thundered the wrestler justifying his cruelty.

"But what has she done?" enquired the inquisitive neighbours.

"What is the need of moving her hips while kneading the flour? Can't she do it without moving?"

Pandit seemed to have forgotten about the fire-wood and was deeply engrossed in the story. He immediately understood the latent essence of the joke, gave a faint forced smile, maintained his seriousness and said, "Chaudharyji, I am not in a mood to listen to your jokes. My need is only fire-wood for the kitchen."

"It appears you have quarreled with your wife and unable to do anything there, you are getting furious with the problem of fire-wood. Come, let us smoke while we try to solve the same," said Chaudhary while pushing the *'hookah'* towards Pandit. The good-natured Pandit fell into the snare, had a few quick puffs and said calmly, "Chaudhary Sahib, I am very serious. The issue is of vital importance and you have to find some lasting solution. Collecting wood is extremely tiring and the smoke of the wet wood has already spoiled my eyes." To support his statement, he opened his right eye wide open with the fingers of his two hands.

"You belong to this village and know everyone. Can you tell me some proper solution?"

"Purchase a dry tree-trunk and I will cut it for you."

"You better try to find out if somebody is selling one. We will buy it to solve the problem for a few months."

Masterji, who was little more apprehensive of the problem and had heard their conversation, asked Chaudhary during the evening stroll, "Fire-wood seems to be a serious and perennial problem here and I anticipate serious crisis. We have to hammer out a solution on war footing. Suppose, we do not get any dry tree-trunk, how shall we solve the problem?"

"You don't worry and keep on preparing for your competition. I will announce this in various classes tomorrow. Some child will certainly come to our rescue."

"The situation is worsening everyday and I fear, Pandit will raise hands one day. There being no *'dhabas'* in and around the village, we will just be stranded. In fact, I would have got myself transferred from here but it is only because of your good company and the time that I can get here for my further studies that I am keen to stay here for a couple of years."

"I assure you, I will solve the problem. You need not get involved in these petty issues."

"Sometimes I feel, no teacher of science or mathematics has come here for the last five years. The pass percentage of class X has never gone beyond eight. If the results do not show a marked improvement, I am afraid I will lose all the respect that I am getting at present."

"Never worry unnecessarily. There is always victory beyond fear. The students are not so bad and you are coaching them even at night. Your efforts will certainly bear fruit," consoled Chaudhary.

Announcements in classes, visits to villages and requests to farmers proved futile. The problem still remained unsolved. It was not because the people were unwilling to help the teachers and students but dry wood was not available, for the trees were scarce in the area. Getting a full truck load from the city was rather expensive and there was also the question of storing the same in the school. A few days passed peacefully, the dry twigs collected everyday by Pandit serving the purpose. The stop-gap arrangement was, however, not lasting and the problem soon started assuming serious proportions.

Sounding a warning bell in the evening, Pandit said, "Chaudhary Sahib, you are taking it very lightly. I have spent my whole life here and am aware that firewood has always been a problem. You must do something or...we will be forced to close the kitchen."

"Tell me then, what should we do? What is your solution to the problem?"

"There is a log of dry-wood lying in the field of Prem Singh. Why don't you try to negotiate with him and buy it? It will solve the problem for this rainy season."

"Pandit, I am not complacent about the seriousness of the problem. I approached him yesterday and made repeated requests but he declined to spare the log. He needs it for his plough as the wood is quite seasoned."

Ram Kumar, a young local teacher, who was so far playing volleyball with the boys, joined them and heard the conversation. Without waiting for a moment, he asserted, "I have an idea."

"Your ideas are always troublesome and I am sure this brain-wave will also eventually land us in some serious problem," intruded Chaudhary.

Ram Kumar was an emotionally volatile and passionately outspoken teacher. His behaviour was generally aggressive and impulsive and he was prone to take decisions in emotional haste. He did not pay any attention to Chaudhary's reaction and continued, "If you cannot get a thing by request, snatch it by force. Let us try to lift it, bring it here and cut it to pieces before the next morning. Not a trace of the same will be left."

All looked at Ram Kumar with mixed reaction. Before anyone had the time to react to his suggestion, he pulled Ranbir Singh, another local teacher, close to his side. Putting his arm around his neck and his weight on his shoulder, he suggested, "Fortunately, it is cloudy today. It will surely rain tonight and by the morning even the foot-marks will be lost in the expected rain. It is a golden opportunity and we two offer our selfless services for the same. Our services are honorary and we will not charge anything for this good deed." Ranbir Singh seemed to agree to the plan and nodded vigorously in assent.

Chaudhary was stunned to hear the plan of Ram Kumar. He was annoyingly blunt and furiously screamed at him. "This is utter nonsense. How can you afford to even think of such a nefarious plan? Is this the ideal that we are going to place before the children?"

Ram Kumar became more aggressive in his reaction and said, "When the belly is empty, all ideals are thrown to dogs. Either accept my suggestion or perish with your idealism."

Chaudhary was highly enraged and reacted sharply with a gesture of defiance, "I will prefer to die rather than resort to such a shameless and ridiculous suggestion." Though highly irritated by the pungent reaction of Ram Kumar, he tried to control his temper to avoid any unpleasant situation and then continued, "We are thankful to you for your offer, but we will prefer to solve the problem in some more dignified way."

"Your outrage is genuine and I will not react to it. We have no vested interest and have offered our services without any selfish motive or personal gain. After all, you are our honoured guests here. Moreover, we are so indebted to Masterji for the good services that he is rendering towards the children of this area. If you do not accept our solution then solve the problem yourself. But I am strongly convinced that this is the only solution at the moment. Always learn to grab the opportunity that comes your way. The fruit is falling in your lap and you are running away." Ranbir Singh appeared to be quite forthright in his decision.

Reciprocating the views of Chaudhary and also trying to prevent the situation from being more combustible, Masterji said, "Ranbir, I am tempted to give my comments, which are in no way intended to hurt anyone. We know you have no ulterior motive in helping us. Your intention is highly appreciated, but not the devious method. We feel grievously hurt because our belief in the values is being shattered. We do not want to do something that may leave us agonised long after and undo all the good that we have done here. Lust once tasted leads to more. We can't even think of living here with tattered reputation. You may have more experience of this area but in our philosophy, honesty cannot take a back seat. What can be achieved by soft and gentle handling of a situation cannot be achieved by force, aggression and deceit. We teach the children to be honest and our words must be backed by our actions. Let us try to explore some more dignified solution rather than stay here with tainted faces."

Ranbir Singh maintained his calmness and politely remarked, "Your adherence to values is laudable, but they will not solve your problem. We have to be selfish in life sometimes and sacrifice our principles for a noble cause. I belong to this community and know everyone. People here are so selfish, opportunist and self-centred that nobody will help you, howsoever good you may be. If you have plenty, these people will lick your feet and if you are in distress, they will abandon you as complete strangers and will not offer even a glass of water. Personally, I fully endorse the plan of Ram Kumar."

Pandit was quiet but seemed to evince keen interest in the conversation. From his body language, it was evident that he also supported the suggestion of Ram Kumar.

"We are indeed indebted to both of you for the kind gesture of help, but your pressure cannot dent our basic principles of life. Your approach is negative and we will not stoop to such levels of pettiness that bring disgrace to our profession. We would prefer to leave rather than live here with the painful burden of dishonesty on our shoulders," concluded Chaudhary. He further implored, "Pandit, please go to Prem Singh today and persuade him to sell the log to us. He doesn't need the plough this year. He can arrange another log next year. Since you belong to the village, I am sure you will be able to put some pressure on him. They may not ignore the request of a Brahmin."

Chaudhary and Masterji were disgusted with the unexpected development. There was now some lull after the violent storm and both left for the evening stroll. The moment they were out of the hearing distance, Ram Kumar reiterated his mischievous suggestion. "Pandit, I still feel, we should try to help our colleagues. Weather is on our side and we must take advantage of the situation. We will bring the log just now and if Prem Singh desires, pay him the price."

Pandit casually glanced at them and gave a faint affirmative smile. He adjusted his turban, picked up the '*hookah*' and left the scene. His reaction and silence were silent indicators of his consent.

Perhaps with the keen desire to help their friends or out of sheer misplaced youthful adventure, Ram Kumar and Ranbir Singh immediately decided to execute their plan. The sky was completely overcast with thick dark clouds and they were not prepared to abandon this god-sent opportunity. The two immediately left for the spot where the log was lying. They did not meet anyone on the way and none would have suspected them also for their village was on the same route. Both were quite strong and it did not take them much time to bring the log and conceal it near the hedge of the school. Their plan worked magnificently and nature also helped them in their design. Not a soul saw them in their deceitful adventure. Just as they arrived in the school, the sun came out of the clouds and the light became better.

During their stroll, Chaudhary and Masterji had obviously no other point of discussion except the problem of fire-wood and the behaviour of the two local teachers. Masterji was more suspicious about the attitude of the two teachers and told Chaudhary, "Although both of them seem to help us, but I am not very confident about their sincerity. Before your arrival, I was feeling very lonely and isolated. Behaviour of most of them with me was very indifferent. On petty pretexts, they would miss classes and persuade me also to follow suit. Coming late or not coming at all, smoking and whiling away the time in the school were their normal habits. At times, they would mark their attendance even when they were absent. I hated their irresponsible attitude. Checking their unprofessional habits would have meant taming the beast or trying to grow grass on the stone."

"Don't worry now. They are scared of me and will never dare say anything to you. I have been highly impressed by your child-like simplicity and deep sense of responsibility. I love you as my younger brother and will always shield you from these rogues. Faith and not blood is the basis of all relations and though we are not related to each other, we have developed a strong emotional bondage. I am also doubtful of their sincerity. If they are betraying their own community, how can they be sincere to us? But I may tell you, they cannot have the courage to conspire against us or even remotely harm us. In this particular case, I am convinced they appear to be really keen to help us. Anyway, we have to be generally careful of their dual personality."

Chaudhary and Masterji could not continue their discussion for a long time. They decided to come back little earlier. The inclement weather or some latent instinct made them abandon their walk half-way. They seemed to have an apprehension that something unusual was going to happen. Their pace on the return was also faster as if something was pushing them to the school. As they were about to enter the school, Masterji's observant eyes fell on the log lying by the side of the hedge. He was stunned for he immediately recognised it to be the one seen earlier in the field of Prem Singh.

"Look Chaudharyji! What is this?"

Going nearer, Chaudhary looked at the log and then at Masterji. He was completely bewildered and immediately shouted furiously, "Pandit, who has brought it here?"

Pandit walked rather casually. On his reaching the spot, Chaudhary repeated his question. Pandit carelessly looked at the log. He bent down little bit and touched it. He posed to look more keenly as if he had seen it for the first time. He did not utter a word and fained ignorance. With no reaction on his face, he just looked at Chaudhary.

"Your silence is not the answer to my question. Why don't you speak the truth? How has this log come here?" thundered Chaudhary.

"Sir, you are just getting furious and making a mountain out of a molehill. Kindly calm down and I will explain everything."

"I want to know who has brought it here," reiterated Chaudhary.

Left with no other option except confession, Pandit spilled the beans and revealed the truth. With a sense of authority and without any sign of repentance or guilt on his face, he added fuel to the fire. "We will pay adequate price to the owner."

A sense of deep annoyance was discernable on the face of Chaudhary, but he said politely, “We left at that time to avoid any confrontation. I am ashamed of their irresponsible and reckless conduct. They have betrayed our trust. I had told you, we don’t want to adopt such filthy methods. We have to be models before the society and you have tarnished our fair name. By bringing it here, they have further aggravated our problem instead of solving it.”

Pandit was argumentative by nature and refused to bow down. He countered, “But why should we worry? We have not brought it here. Our conscience is clear.” His face still bore no expression of regret.

Chaudhary was highly infuriated and reacted aggressively, “Pandit, don’t try to justify your wrongs. You are stubbornly blind and not trying to understand the gravity of the problem. It is a hollow justification. Our conscience is not clear. We are fully aware of the whole drama and are a party to this episode even if we have physically not brought it here. How can we escape the blame under the circumstances?”

Chaudhary appeared to be in a fix and unable to decide anything. He looked at Masterji and asked, “They have betrayed us so deeply. What should we do now?”

“To restore our damaged reputation, there is only one solution. Let us rectify the wrong without delay and put the log back at its original place before the owner discovers the theft. It will salvage our dented prestige. I am prepared to co-operate if you help me in this venture,” replied Masterji with all the force at his command.

Chaudhary reflected for a moment, looked at the log and then at Masterji. He did not think twice to come to a conclusion. “Yes, I fully agree with you. This is undoubtedly the best course. We must act before it is too late.”

Pandit, otherwise a chatter-box, was completely speechless and had no courage to oppose the decision of the two.

Both Ranbir Singh and Ram Kumar had already left for their homes and even their presence could have not altered the determination of Chaudhary and Masterji. Fortunately, the three students were also not there and had gone to their village to spend the weekend with their parents.

The two teachers lifted the heavy log, each holding one end on the shoulder. Walking in the sandy area was quite difficult. Masterji, who held the rear end, was getting more exhausted and tension was further tiring them both. They kept their fingers crossed, completely unaware of the hostile reception that awaited them at the destination. The light had become better now and the two could be easily spotted by anyone on the way.

"Chaudharyji, there is no apparent reason, but a sense of fear is sinking my heart."

"There is nothing to be afraid of. Fear hinders success. Fear and success are the two ends of an action. You have to choose one. He who is afraid always ends in disgrace. I have not learnt defeat. We have taken the correct decision and God will help us."

Chaudhary tried to change the topic and said, "I have always been telling you, Masterji, the present generation of teachers is less conscious of their duties. There is a conspicuous generation gap and a degeneration of values."

"I agree. The values are sliding down but it is not due to any generation gap. Ram Kumar and I belong to the same generation, but our views are poles apart. Pandit and you belong to the older generation, but do you possess identical views on morality? Values are not the monopoly of any generation. They are more a state of mind rather than a matter of years. They depend upon family background, upbringing, environment and education. The degeneration is also due to the materialistic outlook of society."

The two could not continue their philosophical discussion for Masterji was now gasping for breath. He requested Chaudhary to slow down. Fortunately, they did not meet anyone on the way. The advent of the threatening clouds had forced the farmers to leave their fields earlier. Women-folk had also left the fields with their heavy loads of fuel-wood for kitchens and fodder for animals. The fading sun that had come out of the clouds a little earlier was now sinking behind the sand dunes.

Engulfed with the feeling of fear, anger and pride, the two reached the exact spot, completely exhausted. It was not difficult to recognise the place where the log had been lying earlier because of the difference in the colour of the ground. They had hardly laid down their burden when suddenly someone lurking behind a grove of bushes shouted.

"Who is there?"

The two quickly placed the log on the ground and were just turning back to leave, when a man came in the open and said, "Oh Masterji! It is you."

It appears that Masterji, the only young man, who used spectacles in the village and whose face was towards the man, was easily recognised. There was dead silence all around. The only noise was the chirping of the birds returning to their nests, after the day's hard labour and the rustling of leaves caused by the strong wind. Louder than this entire din was the throbbing of the two hearts. The stranger had come nearer the two by now and appeared to have recognised the second person also.

"Chaudhary Sahib! What is all this?"

The two stepped back a bit and looked at each other. They were completely stunned to see Prem Singh there. His sudden appearance had set a cat among the pigeons. Both were breathless, but Masterji tried to work up some courage and broke the silence, "Prem Singhji…you know what happened…"

Prem Singh did not allow Masterji to complete the sentence and interrupted, "You need not tell me, Masterji. I know what happened. There was no fire-wood in the kitchen. Chaudhary Sahib approached me to sell this log. I refused. Unable to solve the problem, you now decided to steal it and were just caught red-handed. Isn't it the whole story?"

Masterji was furious at Prem Singh's rude and insulting remarks. Staring straight into his eyes and without blinking an eyelid, he promptly retorted, "Certainly not. This is not the truth."

"Then let me know the excuse that you have to offer?" asked Prem Singh. He waited for a while and then taunted sarcastically, "I am sorry. I now understand the truth. You were trying to lift it to guess how heavy the log is."

Masterji was highly fuming from within at the offensive remarks of Prem Singh. He was about to clarify when Chaudhary pressed his hand, indicating him to keep quiet.

Having failed to get any reply from the teachers, Prem Singh looked at Chaudhary and said, "Chaudhary Sahib, what excuse you have to offer?"

Chaudhary did not utter a word. Both looked at the log and then at each other and preferred silence. They were terribly hurt by the outrageous and pungent reaction of Prem Singh. They were well aware that their silence was confirming the suspicion of Prem Singh, but still some inner force seemed to have sealed their lips. Masterji looked heavenward and inwardly prayed for some divine intervention to save their wounded honour.

"We respect both of you for your good qualities. Both of you have raised the standard of our school and all are indeed indebted to you. Since you are the *'gurus'* of our children, I promise, I will not tell anyone about this incident. I assure you, your honour shall never be tarnished in this village. But I must say, such a mean and shameful act was least expected of you two."

There was a sudden heavy downpour. All looked at the sky and Prem Singh ran to take shelter under a tree. The gloomy weather had completely dampened their spirits. Heartbroken, the two walked slowly and resumed their journey towards the school. Nature also appeared to conspire against them and the rain pushed them further on the defensive. Wet to the bone, they did not try to quicken their pace. Their speed was also retarded by the strong wind from the opposite direction. All their physical energy seemed to have drained and they were unable to drag even their own weight.

The rain failed to cool down the temper of Masterji, who was extremely furious. He deeply respected Chaudhary and said calmly, "Chaudharyji, I was completely stunned into shame and embarrassment by Prem Singh's outrageous remarks. Our silence was a sign of our weakness and confirmation of our guilt. Why did you not allow me to tell the truth? What will he think of us?"

"It is an irony of fate that Prem Singh appeared from nowhere. Unfortunately, no divine intervention also came to our rescue. What happened was completely unexpected and one-in-a-million chance. The tragedy of life is what you think right can be wrong. I myself could not digest his remarks and was in a fix. Between devil and deep sea, I could not decide anything. In the corridor of uncertainty, I kept my emotions in check for I realised that it would be pointless to defend ourselves and clarify our position. Sometimes we have to swallow unpalatable facts for the greater good and I decided to suffer in silence."

"I am utterly dismayed at your decision. You are normally so bold and I fail to understand why you lost all your courage when it was needed most. Silence has tarnished our reputation and created an indelible scar on our face. We squandered the chance to prove our innocence." Tears welled up in his eyes, though not visible because of the rain drops on his glasses.

"Weighing all pros and cons, I preferred silence. Silence is sometimes more powerful and a better weapon of defence. I felt the situation was not conducive to justify our position. Firstly, he would have never believed us. Both Ranbir Singh and Ram Kumar belong to his area and caste. Who would have cared to accept the version of a Jat from Haryana and a Punjabi from Jullundur? Secondly, even if we had succeeded in convincing him, other teacher-comrades would have been dubbed as thieves. Our own profession would have been tarnished. In any case this would have not solved our problem for he would have certainly not parted with the log."

"Your explanation is really baffling and I am certainly not convinced by your logic. You have a heart of steel, but surprisingly you were completely on the defensive. Silence was not necessarily a better option and your meek surrender was astonishing. It was essential to clarify our position. Now we shall always be blamed as thieves and I am scared that this stigma will chase us during our stay here."

"Remember, patience is a great human virtue and it always pays off. There is greater pleasure in sacrificing for others. Ranbir Singh and Ram Kumar risked their honour for us and it was essential to repay the debt. In fact, we have done nothing except our duty towards our friends. We have returned their gratitude."

"Sometimes I blame myself for dragging you into this dangerous and unfortunate gamble. I lament the moment I suggested for putting the log back. Sudden appearance of Prem Singh is still a mystery to me. I only hope it was not a deep-routed conspiracy to falsely implicate us and tarnish our image."

"I appreciate your courage and determination for such a bold suggestion. Your conviction to follow the right path, even if it is full of dangers, has further enhanced your prestige in my eyes. So far as the conspiracy theory is concerned, anyone in our place would have suspected it. But I am convinced that no one can dare do this against us."

"I cannot put the hands of the clock back nor have I the power to peep into the future. But I have now decided to leave this place. Are even the basic necessities of life available here? Teachers and doctors are not willing to serve in these villages, making the backward areas further backward. There is only one high school for boys within a radius of five kilometers and for girls it is ten kilometres away. The nearest dispensary is ten kilometres away and no doctor has stayed in the dispensary for more than three months. It is normally managed by a compounder. Even if some courageous people come here and want to stay, there is no accommodation or fire-wood to cook meals. I am determined to get myself transferred or resign."

"Let us not feel guilty and regret our righteous effort. Failure and despair should not diminish our enthusiasm and determination to do good deeds. Let us never be disheartened by failures. Even if the end was humiliating, our motives were noble. We board a train to reach a destination, but on reaching the destination, realise that the train boarded was wrong. Pleasure and satisfaction are in the action and not in the result. Unexpected happenings and unpredictable outcomes are a part of life. On our part, let us not talk to anyone about the incident. We must prefer to remain silent even if provoked or ridiculed by our colleagues or called thieves by the villagers. Truth ultimately triumphs. It can be hidden but not defeated. Solution to some problems should be left to time. Remember, life doesn't go on our terms, we go on life's terms," concluded Chaudhary.

It was complete dark by the time they headed back to the school. On arrival, they were greeted by Pandit who was completely ignorant of the last scene of the drama and had also entered the school almost simultaneously.

"I have solved the problem for tonight." Pandit tried to comfort them with a sense of achievement and glow of radiance on his wrinkled face. The two were too exhausted to even raise their eyes and look at him.

"We cannot see you sleeping without meals. After all, you are our guests. My wife has cooked '*dal*' and prepared '*chapaties*' for both of you," said Pandit while simultaneously showing the tiffin box.

The two washed their hands and face and went straight to the kitchen. There was hardly any discussion during the meals. Chaudhary's hilarious jokes were completely absent. The uncertainty of tomorrow had gripped their minds and both were inwardly engulfed in a tussle between right and wrong.

Pandit coughed furiously to draw everybody's attention and broke the silence. "Chaudharyji, why are you unusually quiet today. At that cursed moment, I also lost my reason and was simply carried away by the suggestion of Ram Kumar. But I assure you, he and Ranbir Singh respect you both and they gravely risked their honour to help you. God will certainly reward both of you for your courage and honesty and I fully appreciate your boldness in restoring the log to its rightful owner. In my whole life, I have never heard of such a bold and courageous decision. I have experienced in life that when one door closes, many more open. I have told my wife, from today we are a family of eighteen and not thirteen."

The two perhaps did not even hear what Pandit had said, finished their meals quickly and Masterji thanked Panditji and his wife for the "very tasty *dal*". While going to their beds, Masterji broke the silence. "Let us move forward and leave everything behind for the movement of life is forward. We cannot go back in time as it has no back gear." He had suddenly turned very optimistic in his behaviour. Chaudhary maintained his perfect silence with a faint smile that flew over his thick dry lips, which further deepened the wrinkles on his face. He sensed something more in the optimism of Masterji, fearing if it was an indication of his determination of a new chapter in life, leaving the dry sands for some greener pastures.

❐

4
To Let

Perhaps the most embarrassing thing for me in life has been to prove and justify in a short span of a few minutes that I have always been and still continue to be a gentleman and have lived a virtuous and upright life. I had never realised how difficult it was to convincingly prove over a cup of tea that I had never cheated anyone and had always kept my promises. I had to defend that I always cherished and dearly adorned the noble values of life and firmly stood by the righteous human principles even at the cost of any physical strain or financial loss. This justification, extremely difficult, if not virtually impossible, was required when I wanted to take a house on rent in Delhi, a place where I had been transferred from the calm and quiet sea beaches of Port Blair that had highly enchanted me. My request for transfer to the place of my choice fell on deaf ears and I was pushed to this city of many charms but of fewer pleasures.

This unavoidable transfer was a mix of pleasure and pain. Pleasure, because this was the city where my wife had lived and studied for a few years during the posting of her father. She had also worked as a teacher in a school here before our marriage. But that was about seventeen years back and Delhi had undergone tremendous change beyond recognition, physically and culturally. Picture of this veritable melting pot of Indian cultures, painted now by my friends and the media, was shockingly distressing. The honest man, they held, was feeling suffocated and lost like a needle in a huge haystack. People only murmured a few words of sympathy with no concern for help even in case of a tragic necessity. The wounded were simply left on the road to bleed to death, for the onlookers had no time or were too afraid to get entangled in any legal web. Taking pictures was given preference at the cost of saving a life or honour of a woman. It had been named as one of the most polluted cities in the world. These impressions had further saddened me and I was afraid of being lost in the din of the unruly crowd.

To avoid any loss to the education of my children, I shifted with full bag and baggage and decided to reside temporarily in the guest-house of my office. Fortunately, the grave problem of education of children was easily solved owing to the efforts of my wife. She immediately got a job in her previous school and the children, their admission. Evenings were now generally surcharged with heated discussions in the family and I had to bear, without much retaliation, the sharp volley of arguments. The focus of discussion in the make-shift residential accommodation was mainly on purchasing a house or hiring a better one.

"Papa, it is becoming very difficult to pull on in this dungeon. We have no separate study-room here and there is hardly a living room worth the name."

"You are right my son, but this is the best under the circumstances. You better forget now the spacious bungalows and reconcile yourself to the present situation."

"Why don't you hire a better house or purchase a new one? I am sure you can afford that, papa," suggested my innocent little daughter.

"Everything is available in this world my child, what is needed is money. 'Money makes the mare go' is an age old saying. Renting a house is the only viable option at present."

"You have been in service for over twenty years and still without a house. People normally build a house in about ten years of their service," taunted my son who was in his mid-teens. It was also an oblique reminder of my inability to create a shelter for my family.

Children have a tendency to live in the world of make-shift belief and wanted me to purchase a house by mustering money from 'somewhere' which their innocence could neither define nor suggest. Enchanted by the sky-scrapers, they thought that one could be conveniently acquired by us also.

Search for a reasonably suitable accommodation started. Financial constraints apart, various social parameters had to be satisfied. Safety of the children in the buses (where passengers lacked the social discipline and the custodians due consideration for others), distance of the house for me, my wife and two children, the type of accommodation that we had the privilege of enjoying so far and the minimum that we needed for all practical purposes, were all the divergent factors that had to be reconciled. Considering the various permutations and combinations, the only possible alternative was to hire a house in the vicinity of the school and within my limited budget, purchasing one being absolutely out of my meagre means.

Before coming to Delhi, renting an accommodation was not considered to be a very vital problem. I had never had the chance to hire one and viewed it rather lightly. A few initial failures did not disappoint me although the narrated horrible experiences were simply frightening. In course of time, it proved to be a herculean task. The natural desire of the landlords to increase the rent due to exorbitant inflation and the tendency of the tenants not to pay more due to obvious reasons, led to social and legal conflicts resulting in anything from simple strained relations to court cases and even planned murders. If forced to vacate, the unscrupulous tenants caused extensive damages to the dwellings shaking the little faith of the landlords in their prospective customers. To keep the house vacant, constructed out of the hard-earned savings and with the help of loans from government and semi-government agencies, was not economically viable for the middle-class landlords. Future apprehensions compelled them to look at everyone from a suspicious angle and hence the desire to find a real gentleman. I was confident of an early success though some unforeseen fear lurked the inner recesses of my being.

The first major encounter, a miserable failure, was with the son of a house-owner. Taking a cue, I had gone with my wife and Anil Prasad, a well-wisher and a close friend of mine. A smart young man came out of the house, opened the gate half, but perhaps unintentionally rested his hands on both the gates, indirectly suggesting and forcing us to remain outside the boundary. He was either alone in the house or did not feel like taking us inside presumably maintaining the distance between the tenant and the landlord. The discussion about the house started after a brief introduction.

"Mr. Sharma, we understand that you have a flat in Green Park and you wish to give it on rent," said Anil and, without waiting for a reply, added "My friend has been recently transferred to Delhi and is in need of a house."

"Yes, we have a flat and it is vacant too. We do want to give it on rent and are looking for a decent tenant," said the young man.

"He is a very nice person, a real gentleman. In fact, the whole family is very polished," started my benefactor and used all the good words that his vocabulary could lay hands upon. He reiterated that I was a decent person from all social and personal standards.

Self-praise is no recommendation, but I had to join in to endorse the statements of my admirer and also to supplement a few words here and there, of course, most hesitatingly. It was an exceedingly embarrassing situation for me to hear words of my praise, but I had to stay there for I desperately needed a house. Alone, I would have left but Anil stuck to the situation like a leech.

"Actually, we had a very unfortunate experience with our previous tenant," intruded Mr. Sharma.

"But I assure you that in this case, you shall never have a cause of complaint. My friend's stay in Delhi is not going to be more than three years and he will certainly vacate it earlier, if you so desire."

"So said the earlier one also," interrupted the bold and out-spoken defence officer.

"I just want you to tell me a month earlier and I will vacate the house," I immediately added, supporting my friend.

Sqdn. Ldr. Sharma hesitated a little and then said, "In fact, to tell you frankly, all people are good in the beginning, only circumstances compel them to be different. The previous tenant was an extremely nice gentleman and a very close friend of my father. Since we were not in need of the flat, my father gave it to him after getting possession from DDA. As ill-luck would have it, the gentleman expired after one year. His wife, with three small children, virtually refused to vacate the flat and it took us fifteen years to get it back. Now, whom should we blame?"

Sharma's concern was understandable. My friend did not display any reaction and tried to maintain the same normal smile on his face. My wife moved a few steps back and started looking at the children who were firing crackers on account of the approaching Dipawali. For me, it was difficult to answer as I was myself not certain about my life-span. Evidently, gentleness cannot control our destiny and is not a passport to long life. I stood speechless, thinking about my problem when Anil broke the silence, "You know, Mr. Sharma, life is full of improbabilities and uncertainties and these are unfortunate and unforeseen situations."

"Of course, this is just a stray case. I don't mean to generalise it or prove anything by quoting it. People normally pose to be gentlemen in case of need but actually possess dual personality. Once this so-called gentleman is inside the house, he immediately changes hue and begins to quote all laws under the sky. These days landlords are completely at the mercy of the tenants and to be safe, it is advisable to verify their antecedents and better get some local guarantee. You know, once bitten twice shy."

I was deeply hurt by the offensive tone of Mr. Sharma but managed to maintain my emotional calm. In his fear, Sharma was seeing the image formed in his own mind. Still, trying to convince him, I resumed, "Mr. Sharma, words alone cannot certify our gentleness. You know a person only when you deal with him. I can quote numerous examples of the honest people, but that will amount to pleading my case."

"I didn't mean to say anything about you. Anyway, my father is not at home at the moment. You may contact him on phone. He alone is in a position to take a final decision." Mr. Sharma gave some phone number which Anil noted carefully.

My first experience with an urban landlord was woeful and ended without any positive result. Modernisation in this urban society, I felt, was strangulating mutual human faith at the hands of unfounded suspicion. Those upholding higher values of life were rapidly shrinking to a microscopic minority and were suffering because of the fraudulent majority. Back home, we had to face a volley of questions from children and the incident was greeted with mixed reactions.

The elder Sharma was contacted on phone and he insisted on a known local guarantee. The guarantees that I provided were perhaps not to his full satisfaction and he refused to return the calls. My words and promises failed to create any positive impact on the rigid old man. Frustrated, I decided not to press any further and relinquished the chase. I was still optimistic that the problem would be solved soon.

My search for my desperate need landed me one evening in the house of my distant cousin sister. She was a war widow, and owned a decent bungalow in Greater Kailash. She was an extremely polite, helpful and courteous lady who had seen difficult days and was easily moved by our pressing problem. She immediately offered two rooms on the second floor of her house till I could get a satisfactory accommodation. She was very generous and refused to accept any rent. I was moved by her kind gesture, but my conscience refrained from accepting her offer. She was too good and I was not the man to exploit her goodness.

Fearing that my wife may be tempted, I immediately replied, "Deepa, we would have loved to stay here with you, but the place is too far from the school of the children. We wish to have a house nearer the school. Let me try and in case of dire necessity, I will certainly trouble you."

"You can explore if the school bus comes to this area. From my side, you are always welcome here." I changed the topic and after a cup of tea, we parted company with pleasant memories. The effort remained as fruitless as before.

"But why did you decline the offer immediately? I am sure we could have considered it as a stop-gap arrangement," said my wife on the way.

"She would have not accepted the rent and I don't want to thrive on the generosity of relatives, howsoever good they may be." I replied without a moment's hesitation and added, "I feel relations remain stronger and more lasting from a distance only. Favours weaken relations." I sounded too stubborn, but my views on these issues were rock-firm and I was not the man to deviate even by an iota. Appearance revealed her not appreciating my decision, but she did not retaliate and we reached home disappointed.

The frustration now began to weigh more heavily on my mind. There was another source which I decided to explore independently. I approached a property dealer. The dealers, probably on the advice of landlords, are keen to arrange the accommodation for persons whose departments could take the same on lease basis. In my case, it was not possible. As part of his commission, the property dealer would charge one month's rent. Payment of a few months' rent as interest-free advance and increase of 10% rent per annum were some of the other stringent conditions. In all such cases, the sufferers were the tenants. After all, supply and demand principles of economics moved the world. The efforts through the property dealers failed mainly on account of the lease condition.

Another effort, after vigorous hunting, solved my problem, but for a small hitch. Due to the income tax considerations, the landlord was prepared to give a rent receipt for half the amount. It may appear to be a minor point, but it would have further strained my purse as receipt for full amount was needed for claiming the meager house-rent allowance from my department. Moreover, any condition that violated the law of the land was not acceptable to me. The quest was again doomed to failure.

My well-wisher was keen to help me solve my problem. He came to me with another offer. His boss was living in a very spacious bungalow owned by him. His children were married and well settled abroad. Though not very keen, he wanted a good tenant, for his wife needed some company while he was on tour. Three of us, an unlucky number, went on this promising exploration.

Mr. Kapoor's servant opened the door and made us sit in the drawing room. No words were exchanged during the next few minutes. We kept ourselves busy by looking at each other or by inwardly appreciating the nicely decorated room. We were suddenly startled when the door that opened into the drawing room was opened by the servant. I was just on the verge of getting up, but realised that he was the servant. The anxious moments, comparable to the few minutes before the declaration of a result or before an interview, passed with some difficulty. At last, Mr. Kapoor came and after a brief introduction, Anil explained the purpose of our visit.

"Money is not the consideration. My only condition is that I want a small family to stay here with us," said Mr. Kapoor in a resonant voice.

I was thrilled to hear the condition for I had a well-planned small family and was confident that my problem would be solved. Anil informed Mr. Kapoor that I had two school-going children, my wife was also a working lady and that most of the time we did not stay at home during the day.

Lost in my own thoughts, I was suddenly startled. "But this is not my definition of a small family. For me, a small family is a newly married couple or a couple with well-settled children."

We looked at each other. My hopes were suddenly dashed to the ground with the strange definition of a small family. I managed to maintain my normal composure and my wife kept on gazing at a painting in vibrant colours on the opposite wall, a small child playing with a group of kittens.

"Moreover if his wife is also working, my wife would be deprived of the desired company during the day, defeating the very purpose of having a tenant. I want someone to give company to my wife for I am mostly out on tours," concluded Mr. Kapoor.

We had a reluctant cup of tea. I was getting disheartened, for the gravity of my problem was increasing. I had perhaps no moral right to blame the landlords. The middle class landlords had bitter experience at the hands of tenants. 'A burnt child dreads the fire' and they looked at everyone with suspicious eyes and quite rightly too. Most of them desired the extra income but hesitated because of the problems created by the tenants. The court cases filed by fraudulent tenants had violently shaken their faith in the tenants besides taking away most of their hard earned investments. The upper-class landlords, on the other hand, were not in need of petty supplementary income and preferred to give additional accommodation to companies rather than to individual tenants. Experience with Mr. Kapoor was unique and I kept on thinking about the employment of women and the changing concept of a small family. Women of middle-class families sacrifice their family comforts and undertake jobs to supplement their income in the hope of a better standard of living. Those of upper-class are naturally not in need of jobs, but consume their extra wealth to seek company at home, in clubs or through kitty parties. The concept of the size of a family had changed from a dozen to six, three, two, and now Mr. Kapoor was advocating an altogether different definition of a small family. With all the tension of search, this incident gave me some cause of smile. I was deeply engrossed in these thoughts when the car suddenly stopped with a jerk. We had reached home.

The night was extremely disturbing and I kept on rolling in my bed the whole night. My mind kept on tossing from one issue to the other. Our gravest problem perhaps lay in the ever-increasing population in spite of our best efforts to propagate small family norms. Most of other problems, including housing, emerged only out of this. The influx of people in already over-crowded cities was creating multi-cornered socio-economic and law-order problems. I wondered if I was thinking of all this for I had no house of my own. If I had one, had I viewed the problem differently?

Effort was in my hands, not the result. Search continued as I was optimistic and believed that there is dawn after every night. Next evening, while returning from yet another house-hunting expedition, I and Anil were forced to rest on the lawns of India Gate. Assembly elections were due next month and there was scramble of mad rush and complete traffic block on account of a rally at Boat Club. We had no option but to stay there and kill time till the traffic situation improved.

"Why should the police not manage to regulate the chaotic traffic during such rallies?" said I while sitting on the velvet green grass and added, "There is an exponential growth in vehicular population in Delhi and the infamous traffic mayhem was another reason for my avoiding transfer here."

Anil had been in Delhi for over two decades and had more bitter experiences. While trying to lie down on the grass, he endorsed my point and said "Vehicles moving at snail's pace during peak hours is a common sight here. Cycle rickshaws, hand carts and slow moving horse carts create further chaos and hinder the normal movement of vehicular traffic on the ever-choked roads. Animals squatting merrily on the roads act as shifting speed-breakers and further slow down the speed of vehicles. On the other hand, reckless driving, road-rage due to flared tampers, and poor traffic sense among the commuters contribute to fatal accidents on the road. The hapless pedestrians, particularly the children and the elderly are always at the gravest risk. Government has to do something on war-footing as the situation may soon spiral out of control."

"Besides this, the pollution level has increased significantly and is assuming dangerous proportions. Young children are particularly becoming victims of asthma and other lung diseases. We act at snail's pace and stand up only when we are in the grave."

Our discussion on the traffic problems was suddenly interrupted by a leader with a *khadi* cap addressing the rally. "...Ours is a democracy and you have the right to choose your own government. Vote for our party and we guarantee that we will change the shape of Delhi in the next five years..."

"The fiery speaker is talking about democracy. He may not be even aware of what democracy stands for. Do you think he understands and sincerely follows the noble democratic principles enshrined in our Constitution?" I reacted sharply.

"The ignorant are dispensers of wisdom today. My bluntness may hurt you, but this city with the seat of democracy, the circular Parliament building, so close to where we are sitting is less democratic. Democracy cannot survive effectively without strong and honest law-enforcing agencies. Unfortunately, these custodians of democracy are pathetically weak and easily succumb to pressure of the corrupt. In this largest democracy in the world, there is also scope for maximum willful exploitation of laws."

Anil's furious aggression was surprising. Backing his feelings, I said, "Indian democracy as a social ethic is under grave threat. It is now regressing into majoritarianism, stealing the freedom of dissenting individuals. It is becoming a tool for convenient choices by the majority section of the society and illiterate masses are successfully dictating policies. Galaxy of self-styled leaders has risen from obscurity to fame and fortune through exploitation of the weak. They are adept in keeping double face and in dramatising high moral standards. They maintain one set of rules and values for themselves and diametrically opposite for the common people."

The leader was heard asserting at the top of his voice, "We assure you, after the elections, we will see that all unauthorised colonies are regularised. No business establishment, wherever it may be, shall be closed. Our brethren from other states have come here to chase their big dreams suppressed in their hearts. They are cramped in unhygienic slums and are sleeping on the pavements under open sky. We are committed to fulfill their dreams. We shall provide a plot to every such family..." This was followed by a chain of slogans of "...*Zindabad*" and violent clapping by the captive crowd.

"We are struggling to get a house on rent and he is promising plots to all. Will he be able to fulfill all these false promises? Can all his assurances be an overnight possibility?" I tried to grill Anil further.

"It is only an election speech; a vote-catching device. It is an age-old stunt to woo the audience and show them the moon. They host meals for furtive canvassing, hire crowds for rallies and transport voters in convoys camouflaged as marriage parties to circumvent any action by the Election Commission. All their promises are futile and the outcome opaque. Did you not hear the cheers that followed his assurances? Alas! All problems of the country could be solved through speeches alone? He poses to be a saviour of the poor. Tell me, is democracy merely a formality to conduct elections? Can a small ink-mark on the left index finger after every five years or even less change the destiny of the people, eradicate poverty and ensure adequate and comfortable living to all?" Anil's face revealed a deep sense of annoyance.

My views on this delicate subject were also more or less identical. I nodded appreciably and added, "It is a subject of sustained and critical scrutiny. The power of the ballot can change the government but not the conditions of the poor. I tell you, the much shouted socialistic pattern can never come through elections alone. The haves have enough to waste and turn a blind eye to the pitiable plight of the have-nots who have nothing to take. The gap between the two has continued to maintain the width if not widened further. You must have read that only ten top Indians hold one-third of the GDP of the country and 78% live on less than rupees twenty per day. The vanity of the elite and affluent is stone blind to these growing disparities and problems of the bottom one-third. Their vulgar display of wealth in this sacred land of cows and saints is alarming. These economic disparities have further deepened the divide and hatred. Surprisingly, every rupee that the government spends, 16 paise or even less, reach the intended beneficiary. It all smacks of poor governance. Only sound policies and proper budgeting, backed by good governance, can gradually change the fate of the poor and stop financial bleeding of economy."

"Take any world ranking index in corruption, poverty, literacy, ease of doing business, malnutrition etc., our ranking in each is pathetically low. Strangely, we rejoice in taking pride in our glorious past, but are not ashamed of our woeful present."

Anil appeared to have deep-seated knowledge of the political system. He continued, "The primary duty of the legislators is to legislate which receives the least attention. They take years to pass a law, but minutes in enhancement of their perks or protecting their fellow politicians against criminal actions. They are constantly busy in exploring avenues for amassing black money. For good governance, they have to effectively run public institutions according to law and with respect to democratic traditions. In such a meaningful democracy, opposition has also to play a very effective and constructive role."

"Opposition in our democracy plays the most negative role. Here it explores avenues to spit venom in the Parliament and often resort to mud-slinging through unparliamentary language. The well of the House becomes a wrestling ring and democratic traditions take a back seat. Their aim is to create chaos and hold the government to ransom through muscle and lung power. Obstructionism is their main aim and they oppose every bill, whatever its national importance may be. Statistics have confirmed that only 10% time is utilised for effective legislation. In turn, the slogan-mongering public blindly copies these leaders and resorts to similar scenes on the road. On flimsy pretexts, they torch public vehicles and destroy national property."

Anil abruptly stopped for no apparent reason. Something on the loud speaker had disturbed him. He looked at me and resumed, "The worst is criminalisation of politics that has been allowed to grow for decades and many members of parliament and state assemblies have criminal charges pending against them. Election campaigns are distorted and huge sums are traded in horse-trading to gain majority. Besides these destructive tendencies, a new culture is developing. The era of coalitions is emerging which is more disturbing and painful. In such governments, we have coalition partners and coalition supporters who have vast ideological and political differences. Their approach is opportunistic and short-sighted, and all these are dangerous signs of endemic political instability. Sworn enemies become convenient bed fellows. Such a relationship is purely tactical and the honeymoon doesn't last longer. The stability of the government is always at risk and power hungry partners and supporters are more concerned about extracting political mileage. Survival is their only concern and in this effort, good governance is relegated to the background. The coalition partners can play a very positive role if they discard their petty selfish considerations. But they tenaciously cling to power and threaten to withdraw on trivial issues, forcing the government to plunge into crisis and ultimately succumb to pressures. The greedy partners resort to amassing wealth through scams and large-scale bribes. The fate of the government always rests on razor's edge due to speculation of mid-term poll. This is highly distressing and a cause of great concern." Anil was now at his convincing best.

For some time, I forgot about my housing problem and responded to this deeply complex and vexed issue from a different angle. "Unfortunately, the opportunistic politicians take recourse to religion, region, caste, creed, community, language and narrow political considerations, throwing the national interests to dust. They resort to appeasement of minorities and backward castes to strengthen their vote-bank. This narrow-minded politics is exploiting the masses and has become a liability rather than an asset to the healthy democratic system. Intolerance and lack of rationality of thought on religion and secularism erodes the very foundation on which our Constitution rests and is becoming the cause of riots in some sensitive pockets. Due to this malaise of intolerance, the world's largest democracy and one of the world's oldest civilisations, has become a barren landscape of brittle mediocrity. Added to this is the sensitive issue of reservation on caste basis. Reservation, which was to become a ladder to climb up to reach the platform of social equality, is being used by some upper castes to climb down and claim 'backward' tag to grab a share in the reservation cake. All these vote-catching mean tactics are weakening the roots of our democratic system."

"Forget about your accommodation problem and join that gang of leaders. You will be a good speaker," remarked Anil sarcastically. "To a great extent, the fault lies with us also. Why do we choose the corrupt and tainted leaders? People vote on caste, religious and regional considerations and not on performance. Public opinion is often shaped by ignomy and polarised views. Abject slavery of centuries has forced us to live in herds and packs. We are moved more by emotions and less by reasoning."

The speaker on the loud speaker was further enriching the list of the hollow promises. "More schools shall be opened in the slums. Education in these schools shall be free. School uniform and mid-day meals shall be provided.

Students from minority communities and backward classes shall be given scholarships besides all girl students. We are particularly concerned about the health of our mothers and sisters and more hospitals shall be established for them. We will set right all wrongs done by the previous government. Give us your vote and we will give you food, clothing, shelter and employment…"

"Anil, I must admire the confidence with which the promises are being made by these hypocrites. People have herd mentality and their clapping shows that they are getting enchanted by the illusions created by the leaders even though they are well aware of the shoddy state of ground realities."

"I am optimistic by nature, but my faith in the system is shaking," said Anil with a little defiance. He seemed to be seriously reflecting on the issue and added, "The frustration among the masses is on the rise. The worrying implication is that it may not result in social unrest. The alarm bells are ringing, if only we can hear them. Activism of the powerful media is becoming significant in this direction. These factors will awaken people though they may not solve the problem. All our social problems have exposed the wider nexus of politicians, police and government officials. They are often accused of abetting crime and receiving money. The corrupt politicians feel that they are above law. They freely abuse privileges bestowed by law and get hardly convicted when involved in scams and crimes. They are also aiding land grabbers to spread their tentacles through a mix of power, money and 'fragrant grease'. The precious treasure of historical monuments is at grave risk of public encroachment. Money and power are becoming passports to immunity. Unfortunately, the honest are heading towards extinction like many other rare species."

"Anil, I share your frustration and do appreciate your deep understanding of the problem. My conviction is that corruption is like termite that is destroying the very fabric of our democracy. Spate of scams is increasing trust deficit in our system. But we must realise that corruption is not only at the end of the receiver. Let us watch our own reflection in the mirror. We will be convinced that we too get easily swayed away, fall prey to petty temptations and offer under-the-table considerations to achieve our ambitious targets. These problems are not new but we are getting habituated to face them without displaying any concern. Our normal reaction is *'chalta hai'*. Who is to be blamed for all this?"

Anil had a very strong background of political science and his reactions were becoming more ruthless. He asserted, "Certainly, we are ourselves not interested in a cleaner system. Laws favouring the poor shall not see the light of the day so long the rich frame them. Let the poor legislate and the rich watch their fate. Sometimes, you don't get your rights by begging, you have to snatch them."

"To lighten the seriousness of the academic discussion, let me tell you a story. In an ancient Arabian city lived a rich man. In the morning, when some beggar came to his house, he would role his hand on his beard and would give the beggar as many gold coins as the number of hair that would come in his hand. One day, a beggar came and, as usual, the rich man rolled his hand on the beard. Unfortunately, there was not even a single hair. The rich man told him, 'Sorry, you are unlucky. There is not even a single hair.' The beggar replied, 'Sir, give this beard in my hand and then see my luck.'"

The anecdote brought some cheer on Anil's face and he resumed, "The story assumes great significance in today's context. The rich frame the laws unmindful of the fate of the poor. They exploit the poor in the name of religion by saying that the poor are born poor and are destined to die poor. Economic disparities are mainly social creations and not divine bestowed. Poverty is a gift of the rich to the poor. How can the rich understand the pangs of poverty so long as they enjoy the warmth of velvet cushions and pose to solve the problems of slum-dwellers in their air-conditioned chambers?"

Some more promises on the loud-speaker stopped Anil and after a few minutes, he continued, "Being new to this city, you may not visualise the gravity of problems like disaster of rising pollution levels, green belts giving way to concrete jungle, unhygienic drinking water, power cuts, day-light robberies, sub-human living conditions in slums, serpentine queues outside ration shops and paralysing traffic jams. Sidewalks are becoming temporary abodes and permanent business dens. Garbage is spilling out of bins on the roads. Posh colonies once are now indistinguishable from slums. More than half the residents in Delhi are struggling to survive in large unhealthy slums. They are all migrants and are creating more slums every day. Rapid increase in urban migration has made India the largest mobile population country in the world. Delhi was a city of seven lakh people at the time of partition and today it is a vibrant cosmopolitan hub of over 20 million. The ever-increasing population has lead to mushrooming of illegal colonies and is responsible for overturning every planning model. The rapidly rising migrant population in search of livelihood has resulted in inadequate planning and woeful lack of living space. All these are bitter truths that we are forced to swallow. There are already warning signals that merit serious consideration.

People cannot be mute witnesses to all these issues and consciousness against them is imperative."

"I wonder if there can be any other system better than democracy."

"The system, I am convinced, is very sound. We have more than sufficient laws for attending to misdeeds. The problem lies in its judicious implementation. Action and sincere implementation down the line are more relevant than further legislation. Democracy is rule of the law and if law fails, democracy derails. Police, the law enforcement agency, is very weak and prone to corrupt practices. They are also low paid with no concern for the improvement of their service conditions. Today our democracy is at stake. It is standing on its head and not on the feet. Its path is uneven and not smooth. We have political democracy today but what we need is social democracy. The need of the hour is to create a new paradigm for social justice. Right to equality is one of the cardinal principles of democracy. It should include economic equality also. Equality, without ensuring reasonable provision of basic minimum necessities for survival, is a farce." Anil was now sounding more philosophic in his assertions.

"I also feel that the middle class, hitherto dismissed as an insignificant segment of the electorate, is emerging at last as a steadily growing class of activism around social justice and as formidable political force to be reckoned with. Besides, a new generation of young leaders is on the horizon." After a little pause, I put a straight question to Anil. "We have been reflecting on divergent problems so far. Is there any ray of hope?"

"To live with the change and integrate with the system would be defeatism and a pessimistic view of the solution to the problem. India's claim to the largest democracy rests on four fundamentals: electoral democracy, Right to Information, judicial custodianship of justice, and the rule of law. The real hope is the infallible judiciary. It is the hallmark of a vibrant democracy and its strongest pillar. It is perhaps the only organ of our system that is still relatively less affected by corruption. The courts have vision and integrity and are striving to bring order to the alarmingly growing chaos."

Confident of the integrity of the judiciary, I had my apprehensions about some issues ailing the legal system. "I do not differ with you but feel that the judicial process is disappointingly slow. Speedy justice is of paramount importance. The common saying is 'Justice delayed is justice denied'. Speed of justice is also reflective of the quality of our democracy. We have the poorest judge-to-population ration in the world, one judge to one lakh population as against 100 in developed countries. There is a massive burden of about 3 crore pending cases in courts and at this speed, it will take 320 years to clear the backlog. Because of this, people are tempted to take law in their own hands. There are instances of hostile beasts of revenge subscribing to deviant culture and mobs openly lynching the culprits. The judicial system is not lax and none can bypass it but is often unable to deal with many instances of criminality due to the influence of power and wealth. Painfully slow judicial process, frequency of adjournments, plight of undertrials and problem of intimidation of witnesses turning hostile under the pressure of power, terror and money are some of the serious areas to be addressed."

Shouting on loud-speakers had died by now and the swelled crowd had started melting. I tried to divert the focus and said in a lighter vein. "Just look at the way the hired slogan raisers clapped and cheered the leader when he said that in another decade there shall be no filthy slums in our city and that nobody shall be seen sleeping on the pavements. He appeared to be a magician and promised to eradicate poverty. I think this was a slip of his tongue; what he meant was eradicating not poverty but the poor."

My remarks evoked a faint smile on the face of Anil. He became serious again and continued, "These leaders are very generous in making promises. For us, they build castles in the air and retain those on the ground for themselves. We will live like street dogs so long as poverty-industry continues to flourish in cosmopolitan cities. The poor and less privileged factions also aspire to move from poverty to affluence but the grim reality is that the poor living in urban slums are becoming poorer and the rich continue to grow richer. The rich-poor divide is widening fast. Suicide deaths in this agriculture rich country are on the rise. Wealth is not trickling down to the poor half of the population and richest 1% owns more wealth of humanity than the remainder. One billionaire is added to the list every two days. My heart bleeds for these poor and destitute and growing inequalities are a signal for grave danger."

"I had often heard the leaders saying that we are now entering the twenty-first century. I could not understand how was that going to bring a magical transformation so long as we do not change our basic policies? I am beginning to feel that we may continue to suffer, sob and weep silently even for another century."

Anil sounded more prophetic. He was terribly optimistic and concluded, "Somewhere in our discussions, we have sounded rather pessimistic. The picture is not that gloomy. Let us not be just silent spectators to the problems we have reflected on. The recovery process takes more time and we have to continue trying. At times, dreams are realised at huge cost. Self-awareness awakens us faster than any external stimulus. The pot of evil is full and the day is not very far off when we wake up to a state of self-realisation. We need courage and conviction to fight for justice and protect our cherished democracy. The challenge for a democracy is not that it will change devils into angels. Its peculiar dignity is to get even devils to do the right thing. There are rays of hope in the midst of the encircling gloom. So, hope can't but float about things changing. India is not stagnant. It is on the path of evolution. It can absorb a limp on the road, but it will not be crippled. We as a nation have always fought to preserve our democratic values and institutions better."

The hired slogan-raising crowd had earned the day's 'wages' and was now rushing towards the buses, throwing their flags, banners and bamboos all over the place. 'Vote for…', 'Shelter for all', 'Our Demand – Food, Clothing and Shelter', '*Garibi Hatao*', 'Respect the Girl-child', were all getting trampled under the feet of the madly running crowd. The banners had earned their cost and new ones will be prepared for the next rally. Noble words on them, however, kept on ringing on our lifeless ears long after the crowd had passed. Tomorrow there will be another rally, another party, another set of leaders, with different banners and slogans. Only the hired crowd will be more or less the same who will get their 'treasure' tonight or tomorrow morning from a different 'contractor'. This will banish poverty of some for a few days till the next elections come.

The shadows had started lengthening on the lush-green lawns of India Gate and the breeze was getting chiller. "Anil, every cloud has a silver lining. Waiting here due to traffic block had at least one advantage. For some time, we forgot our personal problem and got involved in solving the problem of millions of our countrymen." Anil sighed violently, helped me to get up, and said, "Sun has just gone down for a while. It will silently come up tomorrow morning again, peep smilingly through the windows of that circular building and brighten the minds of those who will adorn the benches. For us, it is time to go home and plan our next expedition. A promising tomorrow beckons us."

❐

5
He, She and Me

"Raju my son! How are you?"

"I am fine, Mama. How are you?"

"We are fine here…I phoned you Raju, to tell you that Mishra uncle, you know him, whose wife is my colleague, is coming to Bangkok next week. I have given him your address and phone number. He might call you and visit you."

Rajesh Mishra was working in ONGC and his wife, Shobha, was a colleague of Usha, both teaching in the same school. Both the families had very intimate relations and were neighbours too. Rashmi was Mishras' only child and was two years junior to Rajan in school and also in the Birla Institute of Technology, Pilani. She had completed her B. Tech. this year and had joined HCL at Delhi. From the very beginning, relations of both the families were very cordial and both were very keen to further strengthen their family relations and bind Rajan and Rashmi in matrimonial bonds. In fact, Rajan and Rashmi were also very close to each other and liked each other's company.

On his visit to Bangkok, Rajesh Mishra visited Rajan one fine morning without informing him as their relations were very informal and he did not consider the need of any courtesy of prior information. On ringing the bell of the apartment, the door was opened by a young lady.

"Yes please?"

A little surprised, Rajesh said, "I am Rajesh Mishra. Is it Rajan Khanna's apartment?"

"Yes."

"Who is there?" Rajan called from inside and without waiting for the reply came to the door.

Completely shocked and stunned, he gathered his composure and said, "Oh! Uncle, what a pleasant surprise? How are you here?"

"Hope I have not disturbed you, Rajan. I was staying in the hotel just next to your apartment and decided to pay a visit to you. Sorry for not informing you. Today being Sunday, I thought you will be at home."

"Yes! Yes! Uncle, please come in."

Rajesh Mishra was a little reserved type of person unlike his wife who was very jovial, a chatter-box and full of jokes all the time. He exchanged some family information with Rajan and after a glass of soft drink, Mishra left with scores of unanswered questions in his mind.

Back to Delhi, Rajesh Mishra apprised his wife of his meeting with Rajan. She was equally shocked and dismayed to know about the presence of a young lady in Rajan's house.

"I do not know who she was but she was not Indian. There was also a small little girl, about two years old in the house and I was surprise at their intimacy with Rajan," said Rajesh.

After a little pause she asked, "What do you want to say? Do you suspect that the lady was his wife?"

"I hope not but their relations were quite intimate and both were very casually dressed."

"Had that been the case, Usha would have certainly told me everything. I don't think she would hide such a vital fact and keep us in the dark. In fact, just yesterday she herself opened the topic of Rajan's and Rashmi's marriage." She waited for a few moments and then continued, "May be, the lady was someone else's wife."

"I also think so because Khannas would have never concealed the truth from us. Anyway, you talk to Usha tomorrow and find out the reality. But be careful. Open the topic with great care and without any feeling of suspicion."

"Yes, I will."

Shobha was mentally disturbed. She was not her usual self and could not concentrate in the school the next day. She waited impatiently for their common free period when they usually took tea together.

"So, how was the trip of Mishraji?" asked Usha as soon as they sat in the canteen.

"It was good. It was a short business trip and he could not go around Bangkok."

"Did he meet Rajan?"

"Yes. He went to his apartment to meet him." She was naturally sounding very serious in her conversation. After a moment's wait, she continued with a sense of surprise and suspicion as if searching for something in the eyes of Usha, "There was a young lady and a small baby also in the house."

"What?" Usha was equally amazed.

"That is what Mishraji told me."

"I have no idea. May be some neighbour, or a friend's wife?" Usha replied with a sense of assurance.

Shobha remained little serious and both finished tea without exchanging any more information and went to their classes. However, much against her desire, she could not get rid of the fact of the lady and the baby in spite of her best efforts. Usha did not pay much attention but the question of the lady and the baby kept on haunting her intermittently. She was also surprised at the unusually serious mood of otherwise chirpy Shobha. Back home, she retold the whole story to her husband on his arrival from the office. Though surprised, both took the incident very lightly as any serious suspicion was out of question.

Rajan had suspected that Mishra uncle would certainly talk to his parents. At night, when the baby was asleep, he asked his wife about handling the unexpected situation when his parents would ask him the next day. Kate was aware of the relations of the two families and also the fact that Rashmi and Rajan were very close and silent proposal of their marriage was in the minds of the two families in the past.

"The best at present is to say that the lady that he saw was the wife of your close friend who had gone out for a day leaving her and the baby under your care," suggested Kate to Rajan.

"And when the truth is known?" questioned Rajan.

"We will find out some other excuse and if absolutely not possible to conceal the facts, there will be no option except to tell the truth. At present, it is more advisable to gain some time and allay the suspicion of the parents."

There seemed to be two options. Either tell the truth right then or wait for the opportune time. Afraid of facing the reality and immediate reaction of his parents, Rajan also approved the suggestion of Kate to get out of the problem for the present. Not very adept in making excuses and telling lies, he rehearsed every word that he would tell his mother or father when they would call him up next day, which he apprehended they would certainly do.

For no apparent reason, Usha was very restless the whole night and kept on tossing from side to side. She did not hope for anything serious, but some fear kept on lurking her inner recesses. She got up very early morning and rang up Rajan before his departure for his office. After talking about Mishra's visit, she asked him about the presence of the lady and the baby. Like a parrot, Rajan promptly repeated verbatim the already rehearsed story with utmost ease and confidence. Usha was fully convinced with the plausible explanation of her son and both she and her husband, Vikram, heaved a sigh of great relief. Reaching the school the next day, she immediately revealed the fact to Shobha, more to reassure her and also to lighten the burden of her own mind. All details were discussed during the tea time. Shobha had an audible exhalation of relief and normal cheers and smiles returned to their faces. Both the ladies were fully satisfied with Rajan's version as anything else was beyond their imagination. However, some inner feeling of suspicion still troubled the minds of all concerned.

After his B.Tech. from Birla Institute of Technology, Pilani, Rajan had joined HCL for a few months, but the lure of greener pastures in the foreign land brought him to Bangkok. While trying to gain some working knowledge of the local Thai language, he met Kate. She was a citizen of South Korea and had gone to Australia for teaching Japanese in a University there. Chance brought her also to Bangkok and she became a friend of Rajan in a coaching centre, where both were learning Thai language to improve their future job prospects in Thailand. Soon, both came closer and the result was proverbial love at first sight. Rajan was twenty-seven and she was six years senior to him in age, but in spite of this age difference, both decided to marry.

Rajan was very simple, shy and reserved by nature and his conscience propelled him to remain faithful to Kate after the intimate relations. The matrimonial bond bore fruit and a very sweet and charming baby girl was born after about ten months. These facts were kept as closely guarded secrets by both Rajan and Kate from their parents. Kate, in fact, had never maintained cordial relations with her mother, brother and sister. Her father, with whom she was very much attached, had died of heart failure when she was in Australia. Her mother had hatred for the brown skin and would have never approved Kate's marriage with an Indian. She still believed India to be a land of beggars, slum-dwellers and snake charmers. Later on also, she never talked to her daughter in life and also disinherited her from all her share in parental property and other assets. She virtually disowned her as her daughter. All this was because of her highly arrogant nature coupled with Kate's marriage with an Indian.

Rajan was very affectionate with both the parents and his younger sister but was closer to his mother. On Kate's strong persuasion, he decided to keep the secret of his marriage and birth of the baby as long as possibly he could. Kate was a woman of a very dominating character, extremely possessive, and suspicious by nature. She was not prepared to lose what she had got in life after such a long wait. The fact of Rajan's past relations with Rashmi also constantly haunted her and she feared that Rajan's parents may not force him to desert her. Consequently, she was reluctant to expose the fact of their marriage at least till Rashmi was also married. Rajan, on his part, was always against withholding this fact from his parents, but invariably fell an easy prey to the aggressive decision of his wife.

Mishras were fully satisfied that Rajan had not married anyone but still wanted to settle the marriage proposal of Rashmi with Rajan as early as possible. Usha rang up Rajan on a Sunday morning and told him that Mishras were keen to finalise the ring ceremony and marriage at the earliest. Rajan got highly disturbed and discussed the critical development in the situation with Kate as the cat was now about to jump out of the bag. With no other option available except to reveal the truth, both decided to tell the whole story to Rajan's parents. With tremendous mental pressure, Rajan managed to gather sufficient courage to reveal the truth of their marriage and birth of the child to his parents. He now felt guilty of withholding the secret for such a long time. What would his parents think of him particularly when he had been so sincere and they loved him so much? He felt terribly ashamed and his conscience pricked him. Kate was a woman of strong character and was less disturbed and tried to instill the required courage and confidence in him.

Khannas were extremely shocked to know the facts and could not believe their ears. Such a disturbing development of events was least expected by them even in the faintest of their imagination from their otherwise very obedient and affectionate son. They had no option but to reconcile with the situation though keeping the secret so closely guarded by their son was beyond their comprehension in life. This created a little dent in their otherwise very affectionate relations with Rajan.

"Usha, why did Rajan do all this? I still can't believe my ears. How shall we reveal this to our relatives? What will they think of us and Rajan who was held in high esteem by them? We have lost all the goodwill that we had earned in life." She virtually began to cry and Vikram tried to console her sobs and continued, "I don't know why he tried to hide the truth from us all these years?"

"I presume, it must have been his fear," she said with a choked voice.

"Fear from whom and for what?"

"Fear of our reaction and retaliation." After a little pause, she continued in defence of her son, "Let me be frank with you. I feel he tried to hide the truth as he had always been afraid of you."

"Why of me? Had I done anything wrong to him?"

"May not be consciously. But your authoritarian attitude during his childhood, which I had been often pointing out to you, drove him towards hiding facts, telling occasional lies and even at times being rebellious. Though you never meant but perhaps he inwardly felt that you loved his sister more than him. This feeling, may be unfounded, but seems to have taken a deep root in his unconscious mind."

"But you know how much I loved him and how much I cared for all his needs? Do you think I ever deprived him of his desires?"

"I agree. You loved him very much. But I feel, his natural development during childhood was always under stress due to your outwardly strict, authoritarian and disciplinarian attitude. Due to your fear, I suspect, he always tried to maintain a distance from you and avoided much contact and discussion. He could never retaliate as he was gentle, submissive and perhaps too weak to oppose you. But let me add, your strictness was duly compensated by my love and he often opened his mind to me for which he could never have courage before you."

Vikram very seriously listened to the observations of his wife and deeply pondered over her views which she had never expressed before so openly and frankly. To defend him he said, "I did set some limits for his behaviour and followed them rather strictly but always loved him and was never obstinate for not fulfilling his demands made within permissible limits. I always desired him to be a disciplined child and a good human being."

Fear of Rajan's future relations with him began to hurt Vikram. Somewhere deep in his heart, he began to think if he was in any way responsible for his hiding such an important fact for the fear of his retaliation? Was he responsible for any negative role in his upbringing? Nothing could convince him of this, but perhaps he did play some small role, directly or indirectly. Fear of the future impact of such a habit of concealing facts began to haunt him. Deeply engrossed in such thoughts of past and future, he didn't know when he had a wink of sleep.

The problem of revealing the facts to Shobha began to haunt Usha. She decided to keep it a secret for some time and continued her normal behaviour with her. However, some suspicion began to lurk the mind of Mishras due to lame excuses in the postponement of the ring ceremony. Fortunately, for Usha, Mishra was transferred and with this Shobha also left the school. The problem was solved to some extent and with the passage of time, the matter automatically met its desired fate.

Impelled by the urge to see their grand-daughter and not out of any retaliation, Khannas decided to pay a visit to Bangkok. For a few days after their arrival, Kate feared their negative and hostile reaction, but they never even touched or hinted at the topic of their concealing the truth of their marriage and birth of the baby for over two years, though they did ask Rajan about the details of their relationship. Soon Kate was convinced of their genuine and intense love for her, Rajan and the baby. She was now confident that her married life was perfectly safe and secure and that there was no fear of any separation as they had accepted the concrete reality. She became very affectionate with her mother-in-law, bought some ornaments for her and lot of presents for all in India. She was very shrewd in winning over the hearts of the people and convinced Vikram that in him she saw the reflection of her own father whom she loved passionately. Khannas were also fully satisfied that their son had a safe future and would enjoy a happy married life.

Unfortunately, Rajan had fallen out of the frying pan into the fire. From his father's unfounded fear of authoritarian attitude in childhood, he now came under the intensely dominant character of his wife. Kate started dictating her terms and enjoying the comforts of her social life without any hindrance. She stopped teaching and forced Rajan to leave his job and start some business as the salary was too meager for her lavish living. Metal scrap business, started with the help of some friends, began to prosper. Soon he established a big scrap yard and bought an apartment too. Kate bought a chauffeur-driven BMW exclusively for herself to show her financial dominance in her society. Obsession with looks and dress would keep her glued to the mirror for hours. Proud of her beauty, she always tried to impress her friends and ladies of her social circle with her clothes, looks and diamonds. Children, a daughter and a son, four years younger to her, were left to the care and mercy of nanny and servants at home. Rajan, a very hard-working man by nature with very limited personal desires, was always busy in fulfilling the ever-increasing sky-high financial and other social demands of his wife. Cut from a different cloth, she was past-master in the art of getting her demands fulfilled, and skillfully and cleverly manipulated her docile and extremely submissive husband. He gave her his credit card to have a free-hand for her shopping. She was so possessive and shop-alcoholic that given an opportunity, she would buy the whole world. The business, though good, was not sufficient to manage the majestic aspirations of Kate. Rajan, in his love for his wife and fear of her rude and arrogant behaviour, soon fell into the trap of dubious means to manage the ever increasing expenditure.

Rajan had no business background but was able to do well. The problem was of recovering money from the debtors while the creditors were always after his blood. He was too simple and had not learnt the tricks of delaying payments. Whenever he could not meet Kate's demands due to payments to the clients, she would force him to delay the payments at the cost of her unreasonable expenses. Rajan once opened the topic of his mounting payments to his debtors and this is how his initiation and baptism into the easy and alluring world of petty lies started.

"Always try to delay the payments. If you have to pay one hundred Baht and you have a thousand in your pocket, say 'I have not even a single penny with me.'"

"But how long can you delay like this? This will adversely affect our metal business which thrives and prospers only on faith and trust." asked Rajan.

"Delay payments as long as you want. Make some fresh plausible excuse every time."

"But, how?"

Just for example, say cheque from the party not received. Again, cheque put in the bank. Then say, cheque dishonoured. And so on."

"Telling lie first time is easy but becomes more difficult later, while telling truth is difficult first time but becomes easier later. Why start with something that causes more problems later on?"

"It will never create any problem if you say with conviction. Others will believe only if you yourself first believe it to be true."

After a little pause, and with greater firmness in her voice, she continued, "People 'kill' their grandparents several times to delay payments. You can also do the same if the situation becomes acute and grave. Learn to wrap the truth in suitable layers of excuses and lies. Language of recovery and payment is an art in business and you must learn to master it to perfection."

"I am surprised but how have you learnt all this? You have no business experience."

"From my mother," was the prompt and spontaneous reply. "She always tried to conceal facts and secrets from my father who was too gentle to understand this."

Rajan was still reflecting on the subject when she paused to issue a warning in a threatening tone with her forefinger pointing at him like a gun, "But I warn you, don't try these tricks on me. I will kill you if you lie to me."

He was completely taken aback by her spontaneous and assertive threat and replied with a fake broad smile, "How can the student cheat the master?"

With the unethical support of Kate, Rajan soon mastered the language of recovering dues earlier and the art of delaying payments. Fear and hesitation never engulfed his mind now in making plausible excuses and telling believable lies. Excuses like, "Cheque has been received from the party and payment will be made in two days; accountant is in the bank and is transferring funds; you will receive the confirmation in a few minutes; party's cheque has been dishonoured and it may take a few more days; payment has not been received from the buyer; import container was full of stone and a claim has been lodged with the supplier, etc." became the oft repeated common lies. Not picking up the phone became very common to temporarily postpone some critical situation. Normally, in such conversations, more than required details were given and inconsistencies in the concocted stories were also noticeable. Some smart clients observed absence of eye contact, a fake smile, and contradiction between words and gestures but did not point out due to shear courtesy. At times, unbearable abuses and threats were hurled at him by the creditors, but he soon became thick-skinned in tolerating the same. In course of time, this repetition of occasional petty lies, sometimes told to avoid temporary embarrassment, gives way to a perpetual habit of telling lies leading man to pervasive dishonesty.

Unmindful of the consequences of such dubious means on the future prospects of business, Kate was simply concerned with her demands and their fulfillment. She had uncontrolled appetite mainly for diamonds, clothes, shoes and other products for enhancement of her personal charms and position in the high status society. Soon she had Rajan fully and tightly in her grip and dominance, and started exploiting him to her full advantage. Rajan was too timid and completely lacked courage to be offensive and resist her temptations. He was invariably enchanted by her sweet words and charming gestures. Caught in the web of relations, he always tried to please her with the fulfillment of her exorbitant financial demands. His docile nature and timidity propelled him to maintain and strengthen the sanctity of the institution of family. Kate, unfortunately, failed to understand that lust for wealth and uncontrolled greed always lead to tragic consequences. Her unsatisfying ambitions and violent mood swings became the root cause of life-long family and financial problems. The coming events began to cast their shadow and the outcome of horrible consequences and inevitable eventual doom was clearly written on the wall. Little did she realise at this stage that short-cuts in life sometimes cut short the life and she was herself digging the grave and paving the way for the burial of the business and future of the family.

Greed is an unsatiable human passion and mother of many crimes. Kate's demands became more frequent and assertions more forceful. One evening she came with a diamond ring which she had purchased from the wife of a Sheikh from Dubai in a social gathering and wanted Rajan to pay Baht 4.5 million next morning. Fearing her wrath, he meekly submitted to her demand and sold two containers of scrap the next day, creating a huge dent in his capital. Demand for diamonds of such huge costs began to multiply. With the passage of time, she began to exhibit a strange mental problem and sometimes even went to the extent of threatening him, saying with all seriousness and full conviction, "Give me money or I will kill your children." May be hollow, but Rajan took them very seriously and began to fear initiation of any legal case against him for domestic violence. Unable to tame the roaring tigress, he would quickly lock the venomous tongue with a golden tape. Keeping finances under some check and running them with a firm fist was absolutely out of question under these circumstances. Rajan's intense love for the children was the factor often exploited by her to get her greedy demands fulfilled. Pain of trauma is more severe when caused by people whom you love and from whom you least expect. But she failed to realise that relations that are slave of conditions don't survive longer. Some love relations and nothing beyond, while some love things and nothing beyond. She belonged to the second category. Relations once cordial began to suffer gravely. Her abuses, shouts, violent outbursts, and tamper-tantrums adversely affected the personality development and upbringing of the young children also. Constant bickering at home and one-on-one confrontation about money in the presence of the children created a grave future impact on the young impressionable minds of the children. In the expectation of peace, Rajan was forced to stay on in seemingly unhappy marriage. Already initiated into the dazzling world of lies, he was now not scared to tell lies to save himself from the wrath of his wife also.

Rajan's whole attitude towards life and business had undergone a sea change. Once during Vikram's visit to Bangkok, the topic of lies came up with Rajan. Vikram was very strict and asked Rajan not to resort to these cheap tactics. On his part, Rajan tried to convince his father by saying, "You have no idea of business. You have been in government service and had always been following the principles of truth and honesty. That is the reason of your purchasing only one small DDA flat, that too with loan from the government. Honesty does not pay these days. If you ask me, our education system should hold regular classes on 'The art of telling lies' to make children more successful in life."

Vikram was simply shocked at the assertive and forthright philosophy of his son. He could never imagine that his simple, gentle and honest son would change to such an extent. He replied, "But we have never encouraged you to tell lies during your upbringing and people will blame us for your habit." After a little pause, he continued, "Have your children also picked up that habit?"

"Nancy is more like her mother, but son is still too young to tell lies. It appears that he hates telling lies." In defence of his philosophy Rajan continued, "No business can go without lies."

"But this is unethical. Seeds of crime germinate in the soil of lies. Moreover, it undermines our trust. It is a weakness of our mind and is easily discovered. Besides, lies are like a house of cards. They fall apart in no time."

"It is a matter of perception. The world today thrives on deceit and falsehood."

"It is the conclusion of a weak and criminal mind. Just as it needs will-power to give up any bad habit like drinking, it needs courage to give up the habit of telling lies even on flimsy excuses. Telling truth does not need courage, telling a lie does. To hide a lie, one has to tell ten more. The path of lies is easier in the beginning but lands one in grave problems later on. Truth is difficult in the beginning but it ultimately saves one from untold miseries and personal embarrassment."

To put his father on defensive and off the track, he said "In courts, truth can hang you and lie can save you from gallows."

"That is a different situation. I am talking of normal situations in life. Here, fear is the root cause of telling lies. We try to be defensive and adopt an easy way rather than muster courage to face consequences of telling the truth."

"But it is not possible to tell the truth every time. Moreover, it is not advisable also. Our epics record that even gods took recourse to lies to achieve their ends and win their wars."

"I know...Absolute truth is not possible. But there are petty lies that we can avoid."

"Don't start giving me advice now. I am not a kid. You had done enough to me in childhood." It appeared that Rajan was now getting into an aggressive annoyance.

In his wisdom, Vikram thought it more prudent to stop further discussion and withdrew from unwarranted arguments. Also, he realised that unwanted advice is consumed to the dustbin of memory. He felt that winning by arguments with those whom you love is self-defeating. He was also reminded of the advice of his wife regarding his being more authoritarian with Rajan in childhood which was responsible for the creation of some gap between the two. He was not prepared to widen this gap at that stage of sunset years of his life.

Petty lies in business may be common, but they could still be avoided most of the time. Unfortunately, Rajan's lies were more due to the avoidance of payments. Since the expenditure was surpassing the income, payments had to be delayed and, hence, excuses for the same. No business could survive if expenditure was more than income. In fact, no family can survive for a longer period if it does not manage its expenses within its earnings. The problem arises when one crosses the limit – the *Laxman Rekha*. Vikram often advised him to create some assets, if possible in India, and save something for the rainy day. To fall a prey to the vice of lies and pressure of undue expenditure is always disastrous. It is said:

"Earn a penny, spend a dime,
Leads to grave or to crime."

Rajan's family life was now getting shattered due to uncontrolled expenditure and the uncompromising and arrogant behaviour of his wife. Unfortunately, his wife never played any supportive role financially, socially or emotionally in his life and he was deprived of the much needed and desired normal family ties. This had become a cause of grave concern for his parents. Frustrations and tensions choked his intellect and mistakes began to multiply. With no other mental support, Khannas began to sympathise more with their son and never retaliated even on his more unacceptable behaviour towards them.

By nature, Rajan was ambitious and desired exponential progression of his business. Driven by this nature and pressure of increasing resources, he invited one of his distant cousins to Bangkok from India. Sunil was a strong well-built man of Rajan's age. He was happily married and had two school-going daughters. He decided to leave his family in India till he was fully settled in business at Bangkok. His late father ran a small grocery shop in Delhi. Even with very poor educational background, he was adept in marketing and filled the void in an area in which Rajan needed some support. By virtue of his experience in business, he tried to create deeper trust with the customers which Rajan had almost completely lost more due to his continuing habit of delaying payments. With his efforts and hard work, the business soon regained the lost ground and began to prosper further.

Leaving aside his problem of submissiveness to the impulsive aggression of his wife mainly due to his gentleness and desire to maintain good family relations, Rajan was very intelligent and full of creative ideas. In his ingenuity and unsatisfying urge of exploring new pastures and further expansion of business, he now thought of establishing a yard in London to capture scrap market of Europe, leaving the Bangkok business to the complete care of Sunil. His wife was also enchanted by the dazzling lights of London, though for different reasons, and without caring for the business to take off, she forced Rajan to shift the whole family also immediately. Decision needed critical analysis, but emotions would always override logic with Kate. In her dream of the charms of London, she underestimated the financial risks as business was the last priority in her life. Sunil tried his best to resist his temptation of shifting the whole family, but Rajan was mesmerised by his dictatorial wife and shifted to London lock, stock and barrel. He did not heed to Sunil's sane advice and failed to realise that in business, one is never beyond gravity and fall can occur any moment. The higher you go, the more the pain of fall. For two months, they had to stay in an expensive hotel till the business was established and till they found suitable accommodation to the choice and aspirations of Kate. London was certainly more expensive and it further drained Bangkok resources as business in UK had still to pick up.

With some capital transferred from Bangkok, business was started in London, retaining the same in Bangkok also under the care of Sunil. Under pressure from Kate, a three-storyed bungalow in about 4,000 square metres with twenty-three total rooms was taken on rent for a family of four persons. For the new Land Rover purchased exclusively for her personal use and to satisfy her undue desire, a retired guard from Buckingham Palace was employed as a chauffeur. Children, now in their teens, were put in the most expensive school in London. Not to talk of public transport, she refused to send them to school even by school bus to establish her false social status there. The family began to live far beyond their income resources and the financial problem began to exert more negative influence on family relations.

By nature, Kate was extremely protective and possessive for her children, so much so that she never wanted them to be closer to their father. She had brain-washed them to such an extent that they stopped trusting their father, thinking him to be a habitual and compulsive liar. She had neither learnt herself nor taught the children the science of flow of money and how it works in life. The son was not a spendthrift but the daughter had striking similarities of habits with her mother. She was as abusive as her mother, though the mother was more aggressive in her shouts. Both had an intense obsession for shopping and never realised that money is a limited resource. Each exploited Rajan more than the other and in the competition, life and pocket of Rajan were ruined. She also competed with her father in telling petty lies on some excuses so much so that on one occasion, while in US for her studies, she asked her father for money on the pretext that she had to sell her dress as she had no money for her dinner and was hungry for two days. Kate further exploited such false situations in hurling the dirtiest of abuses on Rajan to which he was not accustomed and had never experienced in childhood. He had virtually become so timid that he often wept alone in his room. Even when not required, he resorted to telling lies just for the fear of saving himself, even though temporarily, from the aggressive behaviour of his wife and daughter. In the dysfunctional family, the relations became more fragile and complicated, and, in course of time, they were completely devastated. They now began to live as strangers in their own big mansion.

The business, good from normal standard, started suffering due to huge expenditure. Ever-increasing expenditure began to soar above the permissible limits of income. Unfortunately, for Rajan, two of his Indian managers, distant cousins in relation to each other, started siphoning money from the company to their own company resulting in further losses mainly due to his absolute blind faith in them. They had spotted the weakness of Rajan and the insatiable greed of his wife and fully exploited the situation. They went to the extent of cheating the foreign customers and started exporting substandard material and even stones instead of metal scarp. Lies were now replaced by cheating, another step above in the realm of crime. Rajan could not change course even after knowing the truth. As a result of the same, the name of Rajan's company was blacklisted in the international market and the company soon became bankrupt. He began to hide facts from his wife, further weakening the already fractured family relations. Once the two cousins faked Rajan's kidnapping by an Italian customer to get his forced signatures on some cheques and payment agreements. They manipulated things in such a way that Rajan was forced to leave London for Bangkok, never to return again. Leaving the family at London, he shifted to Bangkok for the fear of the law.

A new, but more unfortunate, chapter started in the life of Rajan. While the family stayed at London due to the education of the son, the daughter joined New York University in the US. Rajan now wanted to establish some business in India and naturally needed some funds. Vikram had earlier sold his DDA flat and had bought a better and bigger flat in a private society through some bank loan. Rajan badly needed finances for business and Vikram had no option but to sell this flat now and move to a rented accommodation mainly due to the love of his son and the insatiable demands of his wife and daughter. With some more money from fixed deposits a manufacturing unit was established by taking some loan from the bank. Personally, Vikram had no financial constraints on account of his and his wife's handsome pension and some income from consultancy services. The establishment of business in India took a little more than a year and during this period, the expenditure in London and US drained some more capital reserved for business. Metal business needed a huge investment and lot of money was stuck up in the market also as the Indian businessmen and government agencies were more corrupt. Running after banks and private investors resumed and unbearable market interest on private loans further increased the financial problems. Not to talk of loans, even payment of interest stopped after some time.

With global economic recession, Rajan's business was also badly affected, causing string of losses and further frustration. Nancy's studies in US started denting the capital, the profit having been reduced to almost zero. Debts started mounting and there was no money to pay the tuition fee for the semester. Unable to pay Nancy's tuition fee, he rang up the dean of the university. "I am Nancy's uncle speaking from Delhi. Actually, Nancy's father has suddenly died of heart failure and the payment of Nancy's tuition fee is likely to be delayed." Rajan's ingenuity had mastered the craft of concocting multiple excuses for delaying payments. He could now weave his thoughts and words without remorse or any feeling of fear or guilt. He could offer convincing and credible excuses in almost any situation and took recourse to this excuse as grand-parents had already "died". Any contradiction between voice and words could not be detected on phone in such a short conversation. Nancy was unaware of this ploy but, fortunately, no one from the University phoned her for the "condolence" of her father who was very much alive.

Life is a game of snakes and ladders; some are fortunate to come across more ladders while some encounter only snakes. Having consumed all his moveable and immoveable resources to the last penny, the era of borrowing from relatives and friends started, putting all in deep problem of debts. Vikram took loan against gold and borrowed more money in his name. Usha borrowed ₹ 50 lakh from a close relative for the tuition fee of Nancy for the last semester to overcome the grave problem of discontinuation of her studies. The loans taken resulted in serious future litigations due to dishonouring of cheques, which completely shattered the peace of mind and lives of all. There seemed to be no viable and immediate solution to the problem and Vikram was not left with any movable or immovable assets now to repay the huge loans. Accusations, pungent abuses, threats and even small mob-gathering became an order of the day, creating an irreparable dent in self-respect, the last invaluable human resource. The father-son duo began to be dubbed as cheats. The pension of the family now started getting consumed for the EMIs of all the three cars already sold. Selling wares for survival is a sure sign of downfall which was now inevitable. In caring to solve the problems of others, Rajan continued to increase his own. In their love for their son, Vikram and Usha managed to take loans for the payments of his debts and in turn increased their problems. The financial problems initiated by Kate, passed on to Rajan and from him over to Khannas. This became the root cause of the disaster of the two families and its six members. On virtual life support system, chances of any revival through socially permissible limits were extremely bleak. Optimism of some windfall was the only ray of hope as life is always full of unexpected possibilities.

With no visible way out of this maze, Vikram one day implored, "Rajan, how can we pull on like this?"

"What can I do? I am trying my best."

"You have to reduce your expenses. Bring your wife and son here and let him study in India."

"They cannot adjust here and I can't even ask them."

Actually, he had no courage to suggest this even at this critical stage to his wife who was always bent upon squeezing him financially. Vikram still tried to press his point in the hope of some positive effect. "Rajan, we may try to reduce our office expenses to the minimum. After all, penny saved is penny earned."

With a view to stop further discussions on the subject, he violently retaliated, "You need not interfere in my affairs. Expenses have already been reduced to the minimum. I cannot manage with less than this."

"True. But with no income at present, how can we spend about ₹ 8 lakh per month? We are already heavily in debt and are unable to pay even the interest."

"Tell me if you have some better solution otherwise leave everything to me," said Rajan with a sense of frustration and annoyance. This finally brought a virtual end to any further discussion on the subject.

Problem did not lie in income, but in avoidable expenditure. When pushed to the wall, his only reply used to be that he will manage by hook or by crook. Once he asked his sister for some money and she, being wiser, politely refused. She realised that non-returnable loan hurts the finances of the giver and spoils the taker. She was not in a position to give a loan which could be written off. She perhaps wanted to help her brother, but because of the uncontrolled expenditure of his family, of which she was fully aware, she felt that money was too precious to be wasted on undeserving relatives. He retaliated violently by writing to her, "I know gold is heavier than blood." More pungent mails were exchanged and the relations already hanging by a delicate thread now virtually came to an end. Strained relations between brother and sister caused further mental pain to Khannas.

One of the weaknesses of Rajan was to put every problem under the carpet, thinking that it will never trouble him again. He was like the pigeon that closes his eyes on seeing a cat, thinking that the cat is also not seeing him or like the ostrich that buries his head in sand and pretends that hunter is not there. To postpone the problem of payments of debts, he was very prompt to issue cheques, irrespective of the actual position of the bank balance. The result was dishonouring of cheques and piling up of cases in courts. Legal problems began to hover on the horizon and threaten the very survival of life. Arrears of staff salary, electricity bills, phone bills, gas bills, house rent, petty payments, etc., all started mounting. He could never negotiate the twists and turns of life and failed to appreciate that time and money fly very quickly and should never be trusted. He had reached a point of no return and could not go back in time. He had the potential but was always weighed down by failures and his weaknesses. With no solution in sight, frustration further increased shattering self-confidence and lowering reasoning ability.

In pursuit of intense love for children and in the race to help everyone, Rajan lost everything. He often wondered if all this was his own doing or divine bestowed? The root-cause lay in the distant past when he failed to summon enough courage to stand against the pernicious and unjustified demands of his greedy wife and meekly surrendered to her hostile whims. She was then completely intoxicated with her greed and the children instinctively followed her. Her uncompromising nature, volatile expression of greed, and pleasure-seeking ambitions were responsible for all his present sufferings and undoing which his parents had also to share now. He wallowed in despair and reconciled to all the woes silently. Yesterday was gone and was beyond reach now. The wake-up call came when it was too late and all were entangled in the web of legal cases. He failed to resolve the complexities of life and crumbled under his own weight.

On one of Vikram's visits to London in connection with the liquidation of Rajan's company, while waiting in the lounge of Heathrow airport for his flight back to Delhi, a gentleman came and sat on the chair by his side.

Seeing Vikram's boarding card, he said, "Are you going to Delhi?"

"Yes. And how about you?"

"I am going to Lahore."

"Lahore? I spent my childhood in Lahore before partition."

This opened a topic of mutual interest for further continuation of their discussion. The area of his residence in Lahore was known to Babar and was quite close to the University where he was working as a Counsellor. His field of specialisation was 'Adolescent behaviour and family relations'. Vikram was presently passing through the same stage of relations in his life and instead of entering into some random conversation, he decided to know about the views and experience of the man expert in the field without giving him a hint of self-interest.

Instead of going in a roundabout way, he directly asked, "Why do children sometimes feel differently from the actual intentions of their parents?"

"Please elaborate your question a little more."

"I mean, parents sometimes love their children but children start getting a feeling that the parents are authoritarian and have no love for them?"

"It is a great human tragedy. Perceptions are sometimes deceptive and if wrongly conceived, have drastically painful consequences."

"But why do children start having such a feeling and how does it get deeply rooted in their future behaviour?"

"The problem lies on both sides. Parents fail to display and prove their real intentions in their behaviour. Children, on the other hand, in their innocence and inexperience, start feeling that they have been deprived of their desired love. The notion gets confirmed slowly, forming a stone-wall between the two and is a sad cause of complex human relations." A little pause and, "But let me add, it is more the failure of parents as they are more mature and in a position to handle their children properly. Constantly disciplining them to conform to the parents' wishes creates a negative impact on the children. They should be encouraged to be self-disciplined and to explore their own skies."

"What are then the consequences of such a false notion among the children?"

"To save themselves from an authoritarian behaviour, the first signs appear in their telling petty lies and hiding facts to save themselves from the wrath of the parents. This habit soon starts gaining strength as lies save them easily. With the passage of time, lying leads to cheating and blaming others to protect their own shortcomings. Mothers can play a more vital role in checking these habits by being friendly with children as children are more prone to reveal their mind to them."

"What happens if they carry such notions in adolescence or even beyond?"

"If not handled properly in time, children of authoritarian parents develop graver personality problems than mere lying and cheating. They develop serious criminal tendencies, extreme aggressive behaviour, and rebellious and revengeful attitude. In serious cases, frequency and intensity of these problems increases with the passage of time. We must remember that Newton's law of motion, action and reaction are equal and opposite, is applicable to relations in families and society also."

"Do such children carry these feelings and reactions in later life also?" Vikram tried to probe further the problem being faced by him in life.

"It depends on the later life. If family life after marriage is more satisfying, these reactions get diluted or even forgotten, but if, unfortunately, the married life is troublesome then these reactions get magnified and are diverted towards wife and children.. Again, if the reactions cannot be diverted towards them, their gravity towards parents and others in the society at large increases. Some do not mature even in later life as maturity is not a natural consequence of growing age."

I was intensely focussed on the discussion and was keen to digest every word. He looked at me perhaps to see the reaction and then continued, "Such children also develop low self-esteem, resistance to taking responsibility, tendency to shift every blame to others, try to trace the cause of their distress in others when it generally lies in them, become inconsiderate of others, act more impulsively, lack anger management, do not share views with others, can't take decisions, follow persons with more power, are intolerant of differing opinions, have difficulty in maintaining relations with others, try to boss over the weak and inferior to satisfy their own complexes, and propensity to lean on others increases resulting in taking negative decisions. Their initiative and ability to change and adapt to changing circumstances becomes low and they try to prove others to be wrong rather than prove them to be right. Many take to drinking and, in extreme case, some to drugs. The research also shows that they develop obesity as they tend to eat more under stress though some develop the reverse tendency also."

"Why do many children blame their parents by saying 'What have you done for us?'"

"This is very common with the present generation which was absent in our generation. Again this is due to their complex to shift blame to others for their own failures and due to their insatiable greed and for the non-satisfaction of their material needs."

Prodding further, I asked, "What then is the remedy to these problems?"

"The responsibility, at least at earlier stages, lies squarely with the parents. They must try to show and prove with every action that they really love all their children with equal intensity. Desirable actions must be encouraged and undesirable patiently moulded. All provocative actions of children must be patiently tolerated and diverted towards normalcy. Aggression and retaliation are disastrous and cause grave and irreparable personality problems. Patience is the key to the problem. Feeling of deprivation of love in childhood must be compensated by more love by wife, children, parents or others. In fact, it is never too late to mend the fractured relations."

Babar looked at Vikram to see whether he was taking interest in the discussion, and after a short pause, said, "I hope you are not getting bored by all these academic details."

"Oh! No. Not at all. In fact, it is highly interesting and fruitful. I have been immensely enlightened by all the information that you have given in this short span of time. I shall always remember this meeting." In his heart of hearts, Vikram knew that all this was a part of his own dismantled personal life.

"Oh! I was so engrossed in the conversation that I forgot about my departure. My boarding time has been displayed and I must leave now. Come to Lahore. *Insha Allah*, we shall meet again." He got up, shook hands and said, "Introspect on all that I have said. I hope this discussion will be of some use to you." He walked away, looked back, smiled, waved, and went straight to his boarding gate.

This brief discussion with a complete stranger had enlightened Vikram immensely and had given him great inner strength. After his departure, he kept on thinking, why did he say 'I hope this discussion will be of some use to you'. He must have judged from his questions and facial reactions that all that he was asking was actually his own personal problem. In hind-sight, he was convinced that Mr. Babar was a real psychologist and told him all without hurting his self-respect. The brief discussion had a very deep and lasting impact on his future relations with Rajan. Vikram's boarding gate was also displayed. He boarded his flight and felt that the burden on his heart was hugely lightened.

Long after the incident, Vikram still cherished the moments of that meeting and "Patience is the key to the problem" had a very deep impact on his later actions. He started restraining him from retaliation against any unexpected and even painful reaction of Rajan and began to tolerate everything even if he felt highly humiliated hoping that it may bring some change in Rajan's attitude towards him and draw him closer to his heart. All his wealth and property had not resulted in any change and he hoped that sealing lips may repair the unconsciously damaged relations in life when his own family had deprived him of the love and affection deserved and expected by him.

Narrating his discussion with Babar, Usha also reiterated that it was due to apparent authoritarian attitude towards Rajan, particularly during his childhood that he still carried in his mind. Rajan had been steadily getting emotionally detached from him and was the cause of his later inappropriate behaviour. Harsh limits had triggered a resistance and tendency to be more regressive and rebellious. He was perhaps taking 'revenge' from him for what he thought was his due and had been deprived of. Limits set for his betterment had been taken in a different light by him and it was now not possible to erase that feeling. Vikram now often used his wife as medium for any suggestion which he thought was better in the interest of his son and it was occasionally accepted. Rajan once remarked at Bangkok, "I have no problem if Mama stays here for two years, with you there is nothing but tension." During any discussion he would repeatedly tell Vikram, "I am not a child. Do not advise me unless I seek it." Whenever he could not do something that he asked him, he would retaliate, "I don't want excuses. If you can't do, say 'no'". Similar words and feelings were expressed by him against him on many occasions. He always felt that Vikram was more caring for his sister and was prejudiced against him though this was not true. He often blamed him that he loved his sister's children more than his though it was completely unfounded. He used to say, "In life you always told me to bear as I was elder and I always suffered." Vikram sometimes wondered if his overweight was also due to the authoritarian pressure of upbringing.

Parental strictness is perhaps the root cause of children's reaction towards their parents. The pent-up feelings unconsciously react like a spring released after pressure or a prisoner set free from a prison. Their impulsive reactions and uncompromising attitude often hurts the parents very deeply and they wonder if they are actually responsible for all that they did for the future interest of their children. Children often tolerate strict attitude of the mothers but are intolerant and reactionary towards a diverse opinion expressed by the father. Wounds caused by your own blood are always deeper, more painful and everlasting. Ironically, every child feels that parents care more for the other siblings and are prejudiced against him. May be parents should adopt a path midway between authoritarian and permissive. There are, however, no set rules and principles in this sensitive area of universal problem.

As years rolled by, age started having a deleterious effect on Vikram's mind and body. Usha, though very caring, started leaning more towards her son. She began to be a greater support and strength to him in his family frustration and in mental and emotional strength. Relations with Rajan had been swinging like a pendulum. They generally remained strained mainly due to payment of debts which was the major problem for the spate of past blunders. Vikram wondered if he alone was responsible for all his problems or there were others who had some share in creating or expanding them. He often talked to himself, sometimes very loudly when alone in the home to relieve his tension. He always prayed to God to give him years to repay all his debts and have an honourable end. Possibility of this was very bleak but there was still a faint and glimmering hope of optimism as dawn follows every night.

Rajan's personal and family life remained shattered, though there was some moral and emotional support from the parents. Kate had gone to US with her children, leaving behind litigations due to huge debts for the three Khannas. Relations with Rajan were now only confined to birthday greetings with the fear of even this formality stopping any time. She was also soon deserted by her children due to her continuous and unwarranted interference in their family lives. Completely dejected and shattered, she returned to Seoul to pass her days in lonliness.

Balance is the essence of all actions in life which Rajan and Kate could neither understand nor appreciate or follow. Balance in needs and wants, in income and expenditure, in lie and truth, and in thoughts and actions, would have brought more stability in relations and peace in life. In her unsatiable greed, Kate lost the love of her husband, affection of her children and was responsible for the downfall of Rajan's business. To satisfy the unjustified demands of his wife, Rajan lost the business, love of children, peace of the family, and to some extent the love of his parents getting nothing but court cases in return. Khannas lost all their assets, peace in old age, and got litigations instead due to their intense love for their son. Life could not be balanced on one spectrum and resulted in disaster for all. Failure to understand, realise and follow the viable path of balance resulted in frustrations, volatile actions, tongue lashing, litigations, and all the resultant pain in life for all. They all failed to rise above dualities and to maintain a state of informed neutrality for peace and tranquility. Perfection is certainly not attainable in life in this imperfect, complex and chaotic world with imperfect people. The course, goals, and destination in life are not static and are ever shifting. Perfection to some extent can only be achieved by trying to maintain a balance in life. Lord Krishana advised dejected Arjuna in Mahabharta when he was going to abandon the battle against Kauravas, the sermon to become a *Stithaprajna* – strive to be balanced, rise above all dualities and to get ahead with his duty without agonising about the result. The wisdom holds good today and will hold good for all times, in all situations, and in all societies.

❒

6
The Broken String

Gautam Ganguly was extremely disturbed on that night and left the bed half-an-hour before the time-piece sounded the alarm at 4:00 am. His restlessness was because of excessive joy and not due to any physical strain or mental tension. Anikesh, his only son, was an engineer with the Tatas and was coming home that morning with his wife after the birth of their son. The atmosphere in the home was incredibly charged with exceptional ecstasy, for all were longing to see the baby for the first time. Sumati Ganguly and her daughter Anamika were also beside themselves with joy but were less nervous than Gautam who was ready one hour before the scheduled time of leaving home.

The two ladies were painfully slow in getting ready and continued at their own casual pace. Gautam was highly dismayed and expressed severe displeasure on seeing his wife who was still busy decorating her long jet-black tresses into a bun. "How much more time are you going to take? If you continue at this pace I am afraid we will reach the station only tomorrow morning."

Sumati was extremely incensed at the outburst of Gautam. His words evoked a strong reaction and she retaliated sharply. "Unnecessary worry and undue anxiety are your normal habits. There is still one hour for the train to arrive. With hardly any traffic at this time of the day, it will take us not more than twenty minutes to reach the station."

"You are not aware of the traffic jams on the roads. If a VIP has to pass by the same route, we may be stranded or forced to take a diversion, if at all possible. Again God forbid, if there is a tyre puncture, will it not take some more time? We must try to keep a margin of at least half-an-hour," pleaded Gautam.

"Why do you always overreact and look at the dark side of the picture? I can answer all your 'ifs' but that will simply waste my time," countered an annoyed Sumati.

"But why can't you get ready a little earlier," insisted Gautam while staring at his wife with deep annoyance.

Coming out of her dressing room and adjusting the border of her *saree*, Sumiti came closer to her husband and taunted sarcastically, "Since you are ready, you may leave earlier. Who knows, the train may come before time."

Gautam, used to such outrageous and pungent reactions, was bewildered and highly irritated by the comments. He felt miserable at the unexpected reaction of his wife. Pushed to the corner, he preferred self-restrain to avoid any unpleasant repercussion on the auspicious day of rejoicing. He satisfied himself by murmuring, "I had never realised that ladies take so much time in getting ready. They do not understand the problem. By this time, we should have left the home." Nervous and restless, he tried to sit but only to get up immediately. He looked at his wrist watch and put it close to his left ear to make sure that it was running.

"Anamika, how much time are you going to take?"

"I am absolutely ready, papa," replied the young daughter by coming out and standing in perfect attention position right in front of her father.

Gautam patted her affectionately and praised, "My sweet daughter is like her father. I am so proud of you and wish your mother had also realised the value of time in life."

Meanwhile Sumati also joined them and the three reached the station about half-an-hour before the scheduled arrival time of the train. They had hardly stepped on the platform when they were warmly greeted by the sweet voice of a lady. "May I have your attention please. No. 2 UP Kalka Mail coming from Delhi is running one hour late. It is now expected to arrive at 7:00 am. The inconvenience caused is regretted."

"Now tell me, what you are going to do?" said Sumati with a teasing smile on her face. "It is very easy to boss over your wife. Can you order the railways to be punctual? I had told you to check the time of arrival of the train before leaving home but unfortunately no one cares to listen to me."

"Damn these railways. They have lost all sense of punctuality now. During the British time..."

"Now papa, please stop your praise of the British time," interrupted Anamika. After a pause she looked at her mother and continued, "Papa did try to confirm the time of arrival of the train but every time the enquiry phone was engaged as usual. Now let us go and sit in the waiting room. What can't be cured must be endured."

Anxious to ascertain the exact position, Gautam went to the enquiry window and asked the clerk about the arrival time of the train. "Why don't you look at the board? Everything is conspicuously displayed there," was the rude reply of the frustrated clerk. Furious but helpless, Gautam felt humiliated and hurt but did not utter a word. He looked at the board to confirm and heard the snide remarks of the young clerk, "Today one has to educate even the literate."

Back to the waiting room, he was surprised to see the two ladies gossiping merrily. They were completely relaxed and absolutely unconcerned about the late arrival of the train. He could not tolerate their indifferent attitude but decided to control his emotions and quietly sat down on a chair only to get up again. Time would run at its normal speed and not faster as perhaps he desired at that juncture.

The anxious moments appeared to creep at snail's pace. The wait was finally over and the train arrived at 7:30 am. They all madly ran in one direction in a bid to locate Anikesh and it was Anamika who first spotted her brother and sister-in-law. Ripples of joy were discernible on all faces and everyone was excited and keen to hold Shantanu who was sleeping unaware of the drama being enacted in the honour of his arrival. All bestowed their love and affection by kissing him. Anamika was more anxious to take the baby but her mother did not allow the inexperienced young girl to carry the child through the unruly crowd and instead took her grandson herself. The proud grandpa was leading the pack with a '*pan*' in his mouth and the corner of his '*dhoti*' in the left hand, intermittently glancing back to have a glimpse of the sleeping child and to make sure that all were following him.

Back in the home, Anamika forcibly took Shantanu from her mother and immediately remarked, "His features have a striking resemblance with those of '*dada*'. He is his carbon-copy."

The grand-parents closely looked at the child again and were happy to reciprocate the keen observation of their daughter. Anikesh looked at his wife, exchanged a loving smile and proudly raised the collars of his shirt with his hands on his proud achievement. There were rejoicings all around and all were virtually busy gossiping and dancing around the new arrival in the family. During these free moments family matters and welfare of the relatives was discussed in details while Shantanu continued to play fondly in the lap of his grandfather.

Anikesh broke the atmosphere of joy and excitement and suddenly opened a serious topic. "Sukanya, let us ask papa about the point you were discussing with me in the train."

"Yes, I am also tempted to ask the same," said Sukanya while getting up from her chair. She sat more comfortably on the bed by the side of her father-in-law and paused for a while to prepare her mentally for the new topic.

"Papa, we have a difference of opinion about a point and we seek your valuable suggestion on the same."

Gautam Ganguly anxiously looked first at Sukanya and then at Anikesh to know the problem.

"I want Shantanu to be a doctor. It is such a noble profession that one can serve the people and also be well off," said Sukanya, hoping to get a favourable reply.

"Sorry, but I bitterly differ with her," interrupted Anikesh.

"Just have patience and keep calm. I will properly present your viewpoint also." Sukanya did not display any aggression, kept her cool and continued, "Anikesh wants him to join the administrative services."

"Those in administrative services command more power and prestige. They are always at the top level of management and virtually rule the country," justified Anikesh.

"Now papa, what would you like Shantanu to be?" implored Sukanya.

Instead of enjoying the discussion and taking it in a lighter vein, Gautam Ganguly became more serious. To gain some time, he parried the question and waited for others to express their opinion first.

Anamika overheard the discussion and immediately replied, "I want my nephew to be a doctor. There is no doctor in our family. Unfortunately I had no aptitude for science subjects otherwise I would have loved to be a doctor."

"If you ask me, I would like my grandson to play and enjoy. The freedom of choice of career should be left to him. But given an option, I would support my son's decision," remarked Sumati emphatically while peeping out of the kitchen. Her tone was an indicative of a bias towards her son.

Both Sumati and Anamika did not seem to give a serious thought to the problem and took only a fraction of a second to give their final verdict on such a vital issue.

From their body language Anikesh and Sukanya appeared to have consolation of getting one vote each. They now inquisitively looked at their papa and waited in keen anticipation for a victory vote. With a grim face, Gautam continued to hold his face within his palms and was deeply drowned in his own sea of thoughts. Much to everyone's surprise, he pretended to look casual and this evoked a feeling of extreme anxiety from all.

"Papa, why are you taking so much time to give your opinion on such a simple issue?" asked Sukanya by mildly shaking the shoulder of her father-in-law.

"It may be difficult for me to decide immediately. If you want my free and frank opinion, you must give me some more time," concluded Gautam though it appeared that he had something else in his mind and was hesitating to reveal the same. He feigned to be tired, yawned violently and lay on bed posing to have a little catnap. It was amply evident that he was intentionally avoiding a reply which may be agonising to all.

"He is lost in some other world. He decides which way to go after the bus has left. This is the trouble with him. For simple things, he takes hours to decide, but this may take him only a few days," taunted Sumati and requested all to come to the breakfast table.

Sukanya's insight had indicated that there was something else in the mind of her father-in-law and he was evading a straight reply. She was, however, determined to find out the reality. In the evening, when Gautam was sitting all alone in the balcony of the flat enjoying the cool breeze, she opened the topic again.

"Papa, you haven't said anything. Have you something else in your mind?"

"Regarding what?" asked Gautam pretending ignorance.

"Regarding Shantanu's career."

Gautam appeared to be little uncomfortable and said "Oh! I thought you had forgotten the issue." He casually glanced at his daughter-in-law and continued, "My opinion on this crucial issue is very different and you may not relish it. Still, I am tempted to express my views frankly."

"Of course papa, I would love to know your honest opinion." There was an optimistic glow of hope and a sense of relief on Sukanya's face.

"I was just thinking, can you decide the career of your child?"

"Yes, of course. Why not? I am his mother. I have every right to decide his whole future." Sukanya appeared to be increasingly confident and assertive.

"I really appreciate your concern for the future of your son but you have to carefully think of the serious implications of enforcing your decision on the child. Parents beam with joy, their hearts brimming with love and pride if their children adopt the profession of their choice. But suppose if they refuse or have no aptitude or inclination for the profession forced on them?"

Sukanya was rather amazed at the logic of her father-in-law. She was expecting him to fully endorse her view or at least one of the views. Not to be silenced by his argument, she said, "As parents, we certainly decide the best for our children."

"Don't mind what I have said. Frankly speaking there are many forces that determine our future, destiny being the most significant. Parents are responsible for the birth of their children, not their actions. Perhaps these vital decisions of life are predetermined and we are made to tread the traced course. I am fully convinced that we are puppets in the hands of someone else. We are slaves of the stars and victims of our desires. I firmly believe, we are powerless pawns on the chessboard and all our movements are controlled by the invisible hand. Who knows what may be in store for our child?"

"Of course, destiny plays a prominent role in our lives but does it mean that effort has no place? Recourse to destiny alone is a bid to hide our own weakness. As parents it is our duty to provide the necessary environment and groom our children towards a promising career."

"I feel it is a very sensitive issue and it may be too premature to take a decision so early. At times parents are very possessive and get too involved in deciding the future career of their children. Possessiveness can be suffocating and parents' excessive obsession has stronger possibility of causing incalculable damage to the normal mental growth of the child."

He paused for a few moments and continued rather hesitatingly, "Parents need lot of patience to understand their children. Sometimes they become too demanding, blindly refuse to accept the reality and ignore the vital factors that play a significant role in determining the career of their children. It may ruin the child's future or may result in an avoidable tragedy." He took a deep breath and added, "Shall I narrate an extremely horrifying and shameful story that I read in a paper long back? I still remember the shocking and painful details of the tragic and seemingly unbelievable story."

Unusual seriousness was discernable on the otherwise cheerful face of Sukanya. She inquisitively looked at her father-in-law and asked, "Of course, I would certainly like to understand the adverse effects that parental desires can have on children."

"Tongue freezes into silence and heart-beat stops when I narrate one of the rarest tragedies that befell a family of reasonably well-educated parents, stone-blind to basic principles of modern medical science, who, unfortunately, lost both their sons because of their desire to see them become doctors. The younger son was about eleven years, brilliant in studies and always topped in his class. He had an inherent aptitude for science and was tipped to be a doctor. The elder one was sixteen and just the opposite of the younger one. He was below average, had no liking for science but was good in humanities. He was at his best in painting and in creative arts and had bagged many prizes in these areas right from childhood. The frustrated parents could never digest the idea of his becoming an artist. Their worry was what would he earn as an artist? They desired both the children to follow the profession of their choice and refused to realise that children differ in their abilities, aptitudes and desires. The elder son could not even clear class XI and this completely shattered the hopes of the parents. In their foolishness they approached a tantric who claimed to be an expert in black magic. He predicted that destiny of the elder son could change if part of his blood was replaced by that of the younger. The stubbornly demanding parents blindly followed the foolish advice and did not consider the grave implications of this deplorable act. The mother fell into the trap due to her deep faith in the tantric and in the grip of overwhelming ambition, turned a blind eye to the potential dangers. In her ignorance, she failed to realise the disastrous outcome and grave risk of the nefarious act. Without realising the gravity of the tragic consequences, she took the suicidal decision and the arrangement for the transfer of blood was made by the tantric through a nurse. The grievous tragedy was inevitable. The younger son died due to shortage of blood and body of the elder refused to accept the blood of the younger. Both must have screamed for help with tears of helplessness in the eyes of the parents. The tragic blunder not only cost them the precious lives of their children, but also landed them in jail besides facing the ridicule and jeers of the public. Of course, the tantric and the nurse were also put behind bars for their heinous act but that was no consolation for the foolish parents. Both the children would have enjoyed a happy life only if the parents had realised that children differ in their intelligence, aptitude, desires and capabilities. Instead of focussing on their strengths and analysing their weaknesses, they forced their own unrealistic expectations on one to lose both."

"The stray incident seems to be incredible and most unimaginable. How could they foolishly do all these things when both were not illiterate? In the greed to have more, some lose even what they have. Impulsive decisions often end in regret and today it is more important to educate the parents to learn the basic parenting skills."

"Everybody is wise after the event. We are shocked and grieved because today we have the benefit of hindsight. All of us make similar mistakes and pursue ruinous courses even though we are all educated. Moment makes a mistake and life suffers. The ambitious parents physically forced transfer of the unacceptable blood and killed their children and we mentally force the transfer of unacceptable ideas and crush the aspirations of children resulting in their mental demise. It may be easier to handle difficult children but it is more difficult to handle overambitious problem-parents in getting rid of their mental block. Never try to trap the sunrays. You will not succeed."

"I am absolutely shaken and unable to get out of my mind the tragic fate and terrifying end of the children. Authoritative parents or even authoritarian ones ruin the personality of their children."

"If you look around carefully, you will come across many such hair-raising experiences. Stress-suicides among the teenagers are on the increase these days mainly because of the avoidable pressure created by the parents. The decisions regarding the choice of career in case of the girls are all the more disheartening."

"Of course, I am an example. I wanted to do my post-graduation in Chemistry, but could not do it because my parents were against my going to Kolkata and staying in a hostel. I was keen to join a college as a lecturer, but had to bow down before the compulsions of my parents. Perhaps, it was not my fate to live my dream."

"You understand now. There are innumerable factors that determine the careers of children. Incidentally, do you know what I wanted to be?"

Sukanya looked at him and nodded her head. Her eyes were keenly requesting for a reply.

"Music was my passion and I wanted to be a singer. But destiny had willed it otherwise and forced me to be an accountant. My elder brother had taken up commerce and economics and I was forced to use his books lying in a good condition in our home. I am now listening to the music of addition and subtraction," said Gautam and had a full-throated hearty laugh. "Of course, I have still great passion for music and follow it as a hobby", concluded Gautam.

"Your times were different, papa. In the conventional families, careers of children were seldom of vital concern to the parents. They were indeed chosen by chance and not by choice."

"Whatever the reasons may be, the fact is that our abilities, interests and aptitudes were overlooked in deciding our career." He waited for a moment and continued, "Story of Anikesh is still different. Do you know what I wanted him to be?"

Looking keenly into the eyes of her father-in-law and making herself more comfortable in her posture, she said "No, he never told me." Waiting for a few anxious moments, she enquired, "Papa, please tell me. It should be quite exciting."

A succession of past events flashed the mind of Gautam Ganguly and he resumed, "I wanted him to be what I could not be, a great musician and an inimitable singer. I recollect his great love for music, his only favourite toys being musical instruments from early childhood. I took it as his passion for music. Practice sessions were very regular at home and I gave him the basic knowledge of *'ragas'*. Unmindful of any stage-fright, he participated in all school functions. People were astonished at his admirable performances and his musical ability at that young age. He could play on various instruments with equal ease, but his performance on *'sitar'* was appreciated most. People were spell-bound to watch the magic of the little delicate fingers dancing on the strings. I remember the days when everyone would shower his blessings on him and congratulate me for being the proud father of such a talented child. His interest in music was at its peak when on a fateful Saturday evening ..." Gautam could not continue as his voice was fully choked.

This further aroused the curiosity of Sukanya and giving a quizzical look, she said, "Papa, please tell me what happened on that day?"

After a little pause and finding his breadth, Gautam continued "I vividly remember that Saturday when Anikesh told me that next day he would not be available for the morning practice-session."

"Papa, please permit me to play a friendly cricket match tomorrow," Anikesh implored on that day.

"You must focus only on music and practice regularly without missing any session. Remember, I want you to be a great musician. You tell your friends that you are not available for the cricket match."

"Papa, this is the question of prestige of my team and I am the captain. If I don't play, my team will be demoralized. If it faces defeat my face will be tarnished."

"And if you don't practice, what will happen to your career?"

From nowhere Sumiti suddenly appeared. Holding Anikesh's arm and drawing him closer to her body, she intruded, "Why are you always after my child? This is his age to enjoy. Let him go and play the match. You are behaving as if you were never a child. What does it matter if he does not practise for one day? He will put some more hours in the evening." She was very assertive to the extent of being rude.

"Yes papa, I will sit late tomorrow evening. Please, may I go for practice now?"

Gautam Ganguly was terribly hurt and highly infuriated at the untimely intervention of his wife. He had always been too timid to resist her dominance or get into an argument with her. He could not even express his anguish and preferred to remain silent. Being a kind hearted father, he also could not ignore the request of his son. Unable to continue the losing battle, Gautam had no alternative but to push the harmonium aside. A sense of helplessness was clearly discernable on his face.

"You go now...but don't forget to complete the lesson in time," concluded Sumati.

Anikesh immediately put his cricket cap on which he was so far hiding behind his back, proudly showed it to his parents and madly ran down stairs.

"Thank you, mama. Thank you, papa. I will complete the task tomorrow," shouted Anikesh with ripples of joy and deep sense of relief on his face.

Anikesh's mind had started working in a different direction. There appeared to be a sudden shift in his interest of which his father was not aware of. He had recently developed a peculiar fascination for Bruce Lee and had his portrait pasted on the wall, right in front of his study chair. His prime interest was, however, cricket and he was a great fan of Kapil Dev. Gautam was completely baffled at the unexpected deviation in his behaviour. In the evening, when he wanted him to practice on *'sitar'*, Anikesh was physically exhausted and mentally tired.

"You are not taking proper interest in your music lessons and your mistakes are increasing. You know there is a cut-throat competition in the world and you have to work hard to be on the top. As you grow, people will be jealous of you and will try to pull your legs down."

"Yes papa, this is common in cricket also in the form of sledging and bodyline."

"What?"

"Sledging, papa. It is a way of pulling other's legs on the field. I think you are aware of 'bodyline'."

"What is that?"

"Don't you know about bodyline, papa?" Surprised at the ignorance of his father, Anikesh continued. "Papa, 'bodyline' is an example of dirty competition. When England could not check Don Bradman from scoring runs, they adopted the dirty tactics of bodyline bowling, so that the players may be injured while making strokes. It is a very interesting cricket serial."

"Oh! Damn that 'bodyline'. I am talking of *'sitar'* and your mind is crazy about some Don." Gautam was surprised at that weird word. All this was Greek to him as he was completely ignorant of even the rudiments of the game of cricket. If at all, his interest was in foot-ball only.

"Papa, I...I was...only giving an example of...dirty competition."

Gautam was amazed at the interest evinced by Anikesh in cricket. He could produce any record or statistics in no time. On Sundays also, he was avoiding the practice-session in the morning because of 'Sunil Gavaskar Presents'. He would keep on looking at the watch and hunt for some excuse to avoid practice just before a similar serial or a cricket match. Gautam Ganguly was sore at his fast-changing attitude and wanted him to take interest in music and nothing but music.

One day he came earlier from his office and saw his son listening to western music and dancing merrily along with his two friends. To avoid any problem, the friends immediately managed a slip while Anikesh had no choice.

Anger swelled on Gautam's face and banging on the table a sheaf of papers that he was holding, he shouted, "What is all this going on?"

"Papa...I...I had borrowed this cassette from a friend and we were...just listening to it."

"Were you just listening to it or were you spoiling your career? ...Is it music?...This is nothing but noise, chaos, confusion and...madness...I want you to listen to Indian classical music and you are wasting your time over these wretched notes."

Lowering his eyes, Anikesh kept on looking at the ground, occasionally raising his eyes and staring at his father. He did not say anything, but felt humiliated before his friends and expressed his deep annoyance and disgust by taking the cassette and throwing it on the table after his father had left the room. Sumati came from the market at that time and saw her son in a bad temper.

"What is the mater, my son?"

"Nothing."

"Why are you in that temper?"

"I said there is nothing. Leave me alone."

"You are always after him. I tell you, the more you try to compel him for a thing against his wish, the more will be his stubbornness and hatred for the same. I have repeatedly requested you to leave his decisions to him but who can change you at this stage?" Sumiti was stern in the defence of her son.

Feeling that Gautam was hurt by her aggressive remarks, she made him sit comfortably to nurse his bruised feelings. "You should not mind my reaction. I have no intention of hurting your feelings. I know you are worried about his future, but remember he is growing, has his own ambitions, and wants to have things his own way. Forcing your decisions on him will create an unbridgeable void in life between you and him. You have to be more flexible and give him freedom to choose his path. When the shoes of the father fit the son, he should be treated as a friend. He has now grown taller than you and I certainly don't like your scolding him every time."

Gautam felt terribly hurt. He felt that his wife was responsible for spoiling Anikesh by always supporting him even on wrong issues. Isolated, he refrained from any retaliation and sealed his lips. But somewhere deep down his mind, he also realised that words of his wife carried some wisdom.

"Sukanya, history repeats itself. You are now trying to do the same for Shantanu. The mental torture and tension that I had to bear in those days may be beyond your comprehension. I am an extremely sensitive person by nature and slightest disturbance effects me most. Your mother-in-law is a happy-go-lucky type and was absolutely unconcerned about the career of her children. Both parents are equal partners and have to be careful to develop near-identical views about the development of their children otherwise it may lead to conflict in their minds. Left to her, Anikesh would have not been what he is today."

"Papa, please pardon me for being affectionately blunt. Whereas mom was too flexible, you were perhaps more rigid in forcing your decision on Anikesh."

Sukanya's unduly frank opinion, though harsh, did not seem to hurt Gautam. "You are absolutely right, my child. I now realise that both of us were perhaps obstinate, your mother for unbridled freedom and me for a forced discipline. Wisdom soon dawned on me and I decided to approach Anikesh's class teacher for guidance. We held him in great admiration and invited him one day to our home. After a cup of tea, I opened the topic and apprised him of our concern and our inability to take a decision."

"My first reaction is that parental compulsions can be highly dangerous and littered with potential pitfalls. Hasty judgements and imposition of unrealistic expectations thrust down the throats of children invariably result in stubbornness and strangulate motivation, the primary factor for progress. They may drive the child to frustration and cripple his personality. There is already tremendous pressure of studies and examinations and inability to cope with additional parental stress may do incalculable harm and ruin self-esteem. It may create an unbearable pain and cause emotional imbalance resulting in a split personality. Instead, parents have to realise and explore the hidden treasure and be friends and mentors and encourage children to excel in the field of their choice. Give strength to their wings and banish from their minds the fear of flying higher. They will trace and explore their own skies. Enkindle hope and confidence among them. Motivate them towards the achievement of their cherished goal. Remember, childhood is like a creeper. It strives for support in the beginning and then in course of time it gains strength and bears sweet fruits.

Overindulgence of parents and comparison of siblings further creates personality complexes and parents must realise that every child has his own strengths and weaknesses."

"I get your point but as parents, can't we take better decisions about their future?" asserted Gautam.

"A child is not a mini adult. Parents must remember that world of a child is different and he has his own dreams and aspirations. Once these are shattered, frustration boils over and the resultant physical and mental pain may be unbearable. Resistance to understand, appreciate and accept the viewpoint of the child may result in disappointment. Parents have to adopt incremental approach and motivate the children in small doses at every step. To aspire and then suffer failure is unbearable."

"But don't you think we must provide all facilities and comforts to our children?"

"Yes, all reasonable facilities and comforts. Remember, ease and facilities are also obstructions in personality development. Not ease but effort, not facility but difficulty make a man. Road to progress is laid with the gravel of hard work. Those who walk on crutches should never dream of climbing the Everest."

Sukanya had no words to counter these universally true facts and decided to change the course of discussion. "Papa, my question still remains unanswered. What should we decide about Shantanu's future?"

"Remember, choice of career should be the result of a collective thought-process which may involve the parents' opinion, child's intelligence, aptitude, interests and aspirations, and also guidance of counselor and teacher. Parents don't set limits. Children define their own. Role of the parents is to create an environment to allow the individuality of the child to bloom to the fullest and let him live a full and rewarding life. Anikesh was almost a top ranker in science and mathematics and I started discussing his interests with him and his teachers. Considering all these factors, our considered opinion was that he should take up engineering as a career. Music, which was my choice, could take the place of a hobby."

While Gautam and Sukanya were deeply engrossed in the past recollections, they were suddenly startled by the presence of someone.

"Oh Sukanya! Here is Mr. Menon, our neighbour. You place your problem before him. His views on the subject are very radical and form an extreme." Saying this, Gautam left the two to discuss undisturbed.

Sukanya was not very keen to place the issue before anyone outside her family, but out of sheer courtesy, she opened the topic with Mr. Menon.

"My views on the subject are less conservative. I am often criticised by others, including your father-in-law, because of my extremely dynamic decision," began Mr. Menon in his strong mesmeric voice.

The very opening remarks of Menon aroused an interest in Sukanya to know more about his ideas. "Yes, papa told me that you want your son to be a tennis player."

"Yes, I have pulled Ramesh out of the school after class X to prepare him to be a professional tennis player. Our society today is also catching up with the world and offbeat careers are finding a foothold in the country with many unconventional options. Institutes and universities in India are offering such careers and there is no dearth of such options."

"I was completely amazed to hear this. In fact, I just couldn't believe it."

"You are simply amazed, others have ridiculed me. One is always faced with hurdles and hostility while experimenting with any innovative idea. My own parents did not relish the decision and reprimanded me. My in-laws were averse to our choice and instigated my wife. She, however, reciprocated my views and we took a conscious decision to go by the talent, aptitude and desire of our son. Tennis is his relentless passion and he is keen to adopt it as a profession. We gave him a green signal after a very careful and considerate decision. The challenge of exploring and translating his trapped talent into success has further inspired him towards his goal. Remember, it is pointless to pursue anything you are not passionate about, since passion is the most powerful driving force for any human action. The only way to success is to love what you strive to do."

"Uncle, excuse me, do you think a child of his tender age is mature enough to take such a vital decision?"

"Your apprehension is justified and very well founded. Our decision was neither abrupt nor whimsical. This crucial decision of his life was not left to him alone. We took into consideration all the vital factors that go in for the choice of a career, including the guidance of his teachers. Ramesh is a natural athlete and possesses the requisite physical and mental qualities of a promising sportsman. God has endowed him with this special talent and our role as parents is to provide conducive environment and adequate opportunities to nurture the same to its potential and help it blossom to its zenith. The realisation of this talent has to be fully exploited to his benefit and welfare of the society. We, therefore, decided to put Ramesh in a Tennis Academy at Madras even in the face of stiff opposition from some. Ignoring his talent, abilities and desires could have been risky and even disastrous. He was Junior National Champion at that time."

"Not to dishearten you or Ramesh, I am also apprehensive whether sports can be a promising career?"

"Times have undergone a sea change and there is a perceptible decline in the traditional career options. See, modeling, acting, fashion-designing and many others are common careers for girls today which could not be conceived of a few decades back. Similarly, Business Management and Information Technology have opened vast career opportunities for all. Sports have also transformed dramatically and are no longer leisure activity. It is an outdated concept that it can't be a fruitful profession. It has opened fresh horizons and is a very promising career today."

"Discontinuation of normal studies is also too bold a decision and I really admire your courage. I am too timid to think of this and feel there could have been some better option or at least a compromise between tennis and studies."

"Yes, there could have been for others but not for us. Most people may decide a different course but we didn't. Firstly, we believe in excellence. One can pay full attention to one side only and we didn't want Ramesh to be a jack of all trades. Between formal education and tennis, he would have lost both. Secondly, the formal education is not being neglected but is being imparted through distant learning. It is an unfounded myth that sports are a distraction from studies."

Mr. Menon waited for a few moments to make sure that his views were being properly digested by Sukanya. Having been convinced, he continued, "Remember, a lion teaches the cub the skill of hunting and the mother sparrow urges the baby bird to fly but remains inert. The choice of the kill and the direction of the flight are then left to the young ones. You can't gauge the flight of the bird till it spreads its wings."

"I don't dispute your point but rules of jungle do not apply to the civilised human society. A gardener constantly tenders a sapling and cares to give it a proper shape till it is grown. Human child has also to be guided till maturity. Your philosophy may lead to value crisis."

"Your concern is valid but the fear is unfounded. I am certainly not advocating unbridled and aimless freedom which can be destructive. Parents have to keep an eye on the children and guide them where guidance is needed. Children have to imbibe the basic human values which are the basis of character formation. These values are not taught but only caught. Let the child learn to discriminate between right and wrong and he will be able to find his own way in life. Let him learn to deal with stress and face challenges of life with insurmountable grit. In fact, the educational system is not just about textbooks and has to make provision for human values also. Education has to be an investment in child's glorious future. Let me also tell you, intelligence alone does not determine the career and success of a person in life. Intelligence is only threshhold ability. It takes you to the door of success but there are numerous other personality traits that determine the success factor of a person. Family's role is pertinent in this regard besides constant financial, moral and emotional support."

Gautam came in at this moment and was surprised to see both there. "You are still discussing the same topic."

"I may conclude that things are changing rapidly and there is a significant attitudinal change. Traditional norms are outdated and have no place in the society now. Break yourself free of flock mentality and worn out dogmas. Don't have a tunnel view and avoid working with closed mind and shut doors. Give opportunity to the children to decide their own course and reduce their dependence on you to the minimum. Free the child of shackles of compulsions and let him learn to take his decisions. Take a decision, continue the effort to pursue it and leave the rest to God. A wavering mind and an ever-changing decision may frustrate the child and create more behavioural problems. Prepare the child for life rather than force life on him," concluded Mr. Menon and left the stage to the main actors.

"What is papa's final decision?" enquired Anikesh who came now and was quite keen to know the outcome of the long discussion.

"I narrated to her the details of forcing my choice on you. I told her that my meeting with your teacher was the turning point in deciding your career. I have ceased to be a traditionalist and have yet to be an ultra modernist. I want to be a realist. I believe, keep the field open for the child and let him learn to explore new horizons. Let him learn to be a man with desire to excel and not be frustrated at failures. He, who is afraid of loss, always loses. Remember, fear effects onward movement of life. There are, of course, situations when there is no trail visible. Good education and congenial environment in home and neighbourhood should teach him to cope up with such situations. Inculcation of a strong value-system comes to his rescue here. Discuss his interests with his teachers, friends, counselors and well-wishers. Do not come to a hasty decision but once decided, reconcile and then provide all the necessary and needed guidance, and physical, mental, moral and financial support."

"To be frank papa, I am utterly confused. There seems to be no tailor-made solution to the problem," said Sukanya.

Gautam was keen to bring the whole discussion to a logical conclusion. "Out of this state of confusion, true enlightenment will emerge. Stronger desires, if not fulfilled, are a source of great suffering. See that '*sitar*'. It still lies at the place where it was last kept. One of its strings broke in those days and with that was demolished the castle of my dreams. I do not want you to suffer similar mental agony and the child to feel frustrated and develop a sense of inferiority. Have the desires but do not take them to heart if not fulfilled. Live in the present and let the worries of the future not destroy the pleasures of the present."

Violent cries of the baby brought a sudden end to the never-ending discussion. "Sukanya, your doctor-administrator is calling you. His day has dawned. Go and look after his present needs first. We will resume the discussion with him when he grows."

❐

7
A Pair of Handcuffs

The sun-god had been extremely furious during the day and the night was unusually hot. It appeared as if the sweltering combatant summer of Ahmedabad was going to shatter all the previous records. In spite of the fans working at full speed, the sweat was running down the body like a stream of hot water. The cruelty of heat had been forgotten for some time by us due to the absorbing *'Hawa Mahal'* programme of All India Radio. The melodious tune at the end of the programme had just been played and we had hardly got up to stretch our body, when the doorbell rang.

"Now, don't sit down with the visitors. First finish the dinner. I can't see children waiting and dozing on the dining table," commanded my wife while I got up to open the door.

In the dim staircase light, I saw Lalwani and Tomar, vice principal and senior teacher of my school. Their faint greetings and sullen faces aroused suspicion and gave me a sudden intuition of some impending peril. My immediate fear was the safety of a group of school children who had gone on an educational excursion.

"How are you here at this time of night? Is everything all right?"

I had hardly completed my sentence when Lalwani suddenly fell down on my feet and, with choked voice, said,

"Sir, I am completely ruined...Kindly help me... Only you can save the honour of my family now..."

I was terribly shocked to hear all this and managed to lift bulky Lalwani to console him. Tomar was a strong man and he helped me in my physical venture. Having seated them comfortably in the drawing room, I immediately went to the kitchen to fetch some cold water for the two and requested my wife to serve dinner to the children. Considering the gravity of the situation, she readily acceded to my request which normally she would have turned down with annoyance.

"What is the matter, Tomar?"

"Sir, Veena has not come home after her duties and Lalwaniji suspects some foul play by some miscreant."

"Oh! But how has all this happened?"

Wiping his tears, Lalwani cleared his throat and said, "Sir, you know Veena is working as a primary teacher in a local school. Generally, she returns home in time but today she has not come back so far. We are all very much worried."

"Do you suspect any reason?"

"I can't say, sir." Lalwani tried to convey an impression of innocence. However, his hesitation aroused suspicion in my mind and I got an apprehension that he was trying to conceal some vital information.

"Have you informed the police?"

"We have come to seek your advice, sir," interrupted Tomar.

"I think we must inform the police immediately." I insisted.

"Sir, this may bring a bad name to her and also dent the prestige of the whole family," replied still sobbing Lalwani.

"Tell me then, in what way can I help you?"

"Sir, we may make an effort to trace her at some of the suspected places where she could have been taken. This is what Lalwaniji desires," pleaded Tomar on behalf of Lalwani. He also pretended complete ignorance, though I gathered in course of time that he was fully aware of the reality.

According to official records, Lalwani was fifty-five, though his actual age was about sixty, the discrepancy having occurred at the time of his migration from Pakistan. He was a very clever person, though outwardly he maintained an impression of complete innocence. He was able to manage fake smile while hiding his inner emotions and intentions. His wife was a slim, smart and fashionable woman in late-forties and could be easily mistaken as Veena's elder sister. She held the reins of the purse tightly and none in the family had the courage to oppose her decisions. Out of their three sons and three daughters, the eldest son was married and was employed with LIC. Veena was the next. She was a smart, pretty, young girl, shy in nature, and had a physical disability, her left leg being slightly shorter which was clearly discernable. All other children were studying in various colleges.

By nature, I was prone to help others and here also, though reluctantly, I decided to accompany my colleagues and got ready for the proposed expedition for an unknown destination. Before leaving, my wife called me inside and strongly warned me against any misplaced adventure. She had better idea of the Lalwanis as she had been occasionally visiting them, their residence being quite close to our flat. "Don't be misled by the apparent innocence of Lalwani. His appearances are very deceptive and my instinctive feeling is that he is hiding something." She tried to persuade me to make some excuse and said, "I am afraid, your impulsive decision may not lead to some repentance later on." I paid no heed to her intuition even though her predictions and valuable suggestions had saved me from serious problems on some occasions in the past.

We left at about 10 pm on our scooters and went to a couple of houses and lodges suggested by Lalwani. After my persistent persuasion, Lalwani revealed that Veena was deeply in love with one Prembhai Makwana who was working as a clerk in a Post Office. He was a dashing young man with a charming personality and his father was working as a peon in an office. The romance of casual exchange of glances on a bus stand had soon blossomed into an instantaneous and serious love-affair between the two. Prem approached the Lalwanis a couple of times with the marriage proposal. However, they strongly disapproved and violently turned down the same due to his caste and relatively very low socio-economic status. They had even threatened him with dire consequences in case of any further misadventure to woo their daughter.

The night-long efforts to locate Veena proved futile and we returned home by dawn, physically drained and mentally disappointed. Conviction gained ground in my mind that Prem and Veena might have already tied the knot and I persuaded Tomar to visit the office of the Registrar of Marriages next morning. The suspense was lifted and lid blown off. It was confirmed that they had married a day earlier after completing all the necessary legal formalities. The information, though vaguely expected, was a rude shock and a terrible setback to the Lalwanis. The slender hope of bringing Veena back home had completely vanished. Without having a second thought, I clearly expressed my inability to Lalwani for any further association and help in the matter.

After the school time, Lalwani again approached me in the office. "Sir, I seek your help to get my daughter restored to our family. My wife is in deep depression and if my daughter doesn't come back home, she may collapse. This will also have a very deleterious effect on the future of my children. Kindly don't disappoint me."

I called Tomar also and tried to convince Lalwani. "Mr. Lalwani, let me say two things in this connection. Firstly, you know Veena is slightly handicapped and with the passage of time it may become difficult for you to find a better match for her. I personally think you should reconcile with the present and let them live happily now. Secondly, you should rise above caste distinctions. These thoughts are regressive and have no place in our society now. Caste differences and parents' opposition need not be barriers in inter-caste marriages when children are intensely in love." Tomar seemed to reciprocate the first point but did not favour the second one for he was himself a highly caste-conscious conservative Rajput.

"Sir, we have seriously considered all these aspects but my wife doesn't agree. Bringing back Veena seems to be the only option with me. My wife has asked me again to request you for help. She only wants the daughter back. Kindly do something to save our family."

It was painfully obvious that my sincere advice had failed to have a positive impact on Lalwani and it was now futile to push my views further. "I really don't know how to help you at this stage."

"Sir, I am in the grip of the greatest problem of my life. If my daughter doesn't come back home, my wife will commit suicide and my family will be ruined." Lalwani fell down on my feet and would not leave till I promised to help him.

On reiterating my inability to do anything since the two were already legally wedded husband-wife, Lalwani resumed, "Sir, we have conceived a practical plan. You need not come directly in the picture. I have decided to seek the help of police. I have talked to the SHO whose son is studying in my class. I know where my daughter is. I want one personal favour from you. Kindly talk to Prem and persuade him to come to school tomorrow with Veena after the school time. He will have more trust in your words. You may take leave tomorrow so that you are completely out of picture." The apparent determination on the face of Lalwani clearly revealed that he had secretly worked out all the details of the nefarious plan with the police. Tomar also seemed to be a party to this and he too reciprocated the decision. It was evident now that he was fully aware of the romantic alliance of Veena and Prem.

"What will you do?" I enquired from Lalwani.

"Sir, the police will manage to restore Veena to us. After that, we will persuade her not to go back to that boy."

"But they are already married."

"We will convince her for a divorce," replied the confident Lalwani immediately.

"I am utterly amazed at your decision. Will a divorce not be a stigma on the life of Veena and a serious blow to the prestige of your family which you are so keen to preserve? Will this not adversely dent the future matrimonial prospects of your children, particularly your daughters, in your community?"

After a brief reflection, I resumed, "I feel your decision is highly impulsive and fraught with grave danger. Anyway, it is up to you to decide the future of your family. But one thing I must tell you, I will not permit any drama inside the school premises." There was firmness in my official decision.

"Sir, we will just talk to both inside the school and then everything will happen outside. Kindly give him a ring and persuade him to come tomorrow," repeated Lalwani and handed over a piece of paper on which Prembhai's phone number was scribbled.

Being a law-abiding person, I was in a dilemma and reluctant to knowingly take such a dangerous step. After waiting for a moment and some mental deliberation, I hesitatingly picked up the phone against my conscience just to help a colleague in distress. I completely failed to grasp the intricacies of the grave issue at that time.

"Hello! Is it Prembhai Makwana speaking?"

"Yes. I am Prembhai. May I know who is on the line?"

"Prembhai, I am Principal of the school where Mr. Lalwani is working. Can I talk to you about something personal?"

After a little hesitation he fumbled, "Yes. Please tell me."

"I know you and Veena have married and I extend my heartiest congratulations to both of you. I only wanted to say that Veena's parents, specially her mother, are worried about the safety of their daughter. They want to meet you to personally see you both. They will not say anything about the marriage."

"In fact, we both were keen to meet them and seek their blessings."

"I really appreciate your kind gesture as a gentleman. Can you come tomorrow to the school after the school time? This will be a more convenient and suitable place for the meeting."

Cleverly hiding their real intentions, Lalwani and his wife also talked to Prembhai on the phone. Lalwani swore by his children that the family had reconciled themselves and that they had no objection to their marriage. Mrs. Lalwani shed crocodile tears on the phone and desired to meet both to bless them. Prembhai was emotionally blackmailed and persuaded to come to school along with Veena. Convinced of his safety and the pious intentions of the Lalwanis, Prem fell into the unscrupulous trap laid down by Lalwanis in collaboration with the police and without a moment's hesitation, confirmed the meeting. I was completely moved by the sincerity of Prem and prayed to God that nothing unfortunate may happen the next day. Inwardly, a sense of guilt pricked my conscience.

In my miscalculated anxiety to help my colleague and also to keep myself safe legally, I took leave the next day so that Lalwani himself was in charge of the school. I erred in my judgment and did not apprehend the dangerous consequences of my decision of assistance in arranging the proposed meeting. At that time, I got easily carried away by my emotions and the tears of Lalwanis.

The next day, as I gathered later on, an unusual drama was enacted outside the school after the school time. Prem was physically thrown out of the auto-rickshaw which dragged him for about hundred yards. The sordid scene of violent pushes by the plain-clothed policemen and some fist-fight was witnessed by the shocked and outraged public on the road. Prembhai had not come prepared for this least expected planned conspiracy. All his cries and wailings were of no avail as there was none to come to his rescue and support. Veena was thus forcibly brought back home within three days of her legal wedlock.

I was completely horrified to hear the details of the shocking episode and felt the grave injustice done to the true and sincere lover. Inwardly, I felt morally guilty of being a party to the conspiracy to the extent of arranging the meeting and not trying to stop Lalwani from calling the police. However, my sincere efforts to convince him to let the children live happily after marriage and the absence of my direct involvement in the case were of some personal consolation.

I did not hear much after that except that Veena had stopped going to her school, was living happily with her parents and that she had reconciled herself to a divorce. I thought the problem was finally over but my optimism was grossly misplaced. I was unaware of the impending gloom and the tragic storm round the corner that was threatening to blow up my fair name and career.

One month after the restoration of Veena to her parents, I received summons from the court accusing me under sections 363, 378, 420 and 120B of IPC for corroborating to kidnap a legally wedded woman, decamping with her ornaments and other valuables, cheating, and for criminal conspiracy. The ground slipped from under my feet due to the terribly shocking charges. For the fear of causing any dent to my self-respect, I was reluctant to seek advice from any quarter.

"I have always been telling you, fools rush in where angels fear to tread. Now reap what you have sown," said my wife on getting information about the summons.

"It is absolutely false and utterly baseless. The story of kidnapping and decamping with ornaments and valuables is only a concoction. Nothing like this has happened and you know I am not at all concerned with this."

"Who is going to listen to you? If your involvement is established in the court, the shame and stigma shall completely tarnish our social image besides conviction and a sure loss of a prestigious job."

"But how can my involvement be established?"

"By producing false witnesses," was the prompt prophecy of my wife. "Who bothers about the truth in this crippled judicial system? Truth is not more important. What appears to be true in the court is more important. False witnesses can be conveniently bought to put the innocent to the gallows. The keys of conviction are in the hands of the witnesses."

My wife's fear and prophetic words kept on ringing in my ears. I was terribly upset and could not sleep for days. Lalwani and his wife had also received similar summons. They were obviously less disturbed as their primary objective of getting their daughter back had been achieved. They had already decided their course of action and were prepared for the worst. On my part, I tried to approach Prembhai to know his intentions.

"You may not be directly involved but I am fully convinced that you are certainly a party to this crime and are instrumental in organising the police action resulting in our separation," said Prembhai with utmost conviction.

"I assure you we have no role in calling the police. We had no intention of separating you from Veena, On the other hand, we heartily support love marriages and inter-caste relations," intervened my wife who was also with me.

"There is absolutely no doubt in my mind that you are responsible for ruining my married life and all this would have not been possible without your active support. You broke the trust I reposed in you and have caused all the pain that I am suffering. Morally and legally, your action is not justified."

"Your false accusations are also equally unjustified from any angle?" asserted my wife.

Prembhai appeared to be highly aggrieved due to his separation from Veena and replied without mincing words,

"We will see all this in the court. I want Veena back and this is possible only by implicating you. Pressure on you will certainly help me achieve my objective. I am prepared to withdraw the case only and only if Veena comes back."

Both I and my wife tried to convince Prem that it will not be possible for him to prove my involvement but all our arguments fell on deaf ears. Shaken inside, I displayed a sense of outward strength lest my fear may make the adversary stronger. The bruised man had his own strong reasons for trapping me in the case and even a disguised threat of action for falsely implicating me failed to have any impact on him.

Days rolled by and court appearances became a routine affair. The problem was taken rather lightly by me in the beginning as my gut feeling was that it will not be possible for Prem to establish my role in the case. I even did not engage my own lawyer thinking that the one engaged by Lalwanis would be able to plead on my behalf also.

The gravity of the consequences became apparent on the day when Prem's first witness appeared in the court. From his uniform he looked like a cab-driver. Prem's lawyer directed him to the witness box and asked, "What is your name? What do you do to earn your livelihood?

"Sir, my name is Dhirubhai Makwana. I am an auto-rickshaw driver."

Pointing towards me, the lawyer resumed, "Do you recognise that gentleman wearing spectacles?"

"Yes sir."

"Where did you see him?"

"Sir, about two months back, he had followed on scooter my auto-rickshaw in which this old man and that lady were sitting," said the driver pointing towards Lalwani and his wife. To my utter surprise, the cab driver gave the correct registration number and colour of my scooter also.

"Can you describe what happened on that day?"

"Sir, the old man and the woman hired my auto-rickshaw from Navrang Pura for Kalupur. This bespectacled man followed us on a scooter. I was asked to stop in front of a house. Both the men discussed something in English which I could not understand. The two then went upstairs while the lady remained seated in the auto-rickshaw. In about ten minutes both the men came back with a girl and a small suitcase which was in the hands of the bespectacled man," said the never-seen-earlier driver with utmost ease and confidence.

"Were they quiet or talking?"

"Sir, the girl and the old man were talking very loudly in Sindhi, which I could comprehend only partly. The girl was trying to go back upstairs saying that she was not prepared to go while the old man was pulling her. Both the men finally managed to push the girl into the auto and she was squeezed in between the man and the woman. The suitcase was also put in the auto and I was asked to return to Navrang Pura. The bespectacled man followed us again on the scooter."

"Thank you very much. Your witness, please," concluded Prem's lawyer while turning towards Lalwani's lawyer.

Unable to rebuff or counter the charge at that time, Lalwani's lawyer pleaded, "My lord, I may be permitted to interrogate and cross-examine him at some later stage."

The false assertions of the auto-rickshaw driver were the greatest shock of my life and his unwavering and strong disposition completely shook me. I was totally taken aback by the ease and confidence with which the driver gave the absolutely false evidence. The unbelievable and potentially threatening evidence was a terrible setback. My hope of getting out of the problem was already bleak and was now further splintered. It brought me to the waking reality that the game had virtually slipped out of my hands. My conviction in the case appeared to be a foregone conclusion. It further tightened the noose around my neck and my fate appeared to be finally sealed. I had always been mortally scared of police and court and both began to frighten me now. I looked at my delicate wrists and began to feel the heavy weight of the pair of handcuffs hanging in the court-room on a peg in the wall.

Outside the court-room, wild jubilation of Prem Makwana was evident. He was overwhelmed with joy and was on top of the world as it had further boosted his confidence of getting back Veena. The pungent and offensive remarks of a handful of his supporters and relatives against me were shocking and unbearable. I had no courage to share my inner feelings with anyone and immediately decided to engage an independent lawyer. A well-wisher introduced me to Mr. Chawla, a noted criminal lawyer of Ahmedabad.

"Just tell me the whole truth and see that you don't try to hide any fact. It will be very difficult for me to save you from the disastrous consequences if you keep me in the dark," said Mr. Chawla during our first meeting in his chamber.

"Chawlaji, I will tell you the complete truth. Otherwise also I am not in the habit of telling a lie even at the risk of grave loss."

All details of the case known to me were sincerely narrated. The reactions appeared to have convinced the lawyer of my innocence and that the evidence produced by Prembhai was false and fabricated. He, however, repeatedly told me that I should have not involved myself even to the extent I had done and also that I should have engaged a lawyer much earlier.

"I really appreciate your frankness. You appear to be quite innocent and transparent. Perhaps your keenness to help your colleague has landed you in such a grave situation. I am surprised that you have failed to judge the magnitude of the problem and the gravity of the situation. Consequences of the case can be disastrous and may entail great deal of suffering to your family. One more such evidence can certainly ruin your complete life and career."

"But how can people give false evidence? Is it not for the law to judge the truth and veracity of the evidence?"

"Justice itself is completely blind and dumb too. It is only a product of the evidences produced. It tries to probe the truth as revealed by the witnesses and other evidences presented in the court. It has, of course, loopholes which abusers and offenders exploit either to get away with crime or to harass the innocent."

"I am getting disappointed about the visible hollowness of our judicial system. The innocent may be hanged and the outlaws may go scot-free."

"The system has certainly its own deficiencies but nothing better can perhaps replace it. Wheels of justice grind notoriously slow and because of legal complications, such cases may linger on for years and one may get only dates and frustration. I am not trying to frighten you but the verdict can be disastrous." Chawla paused for a while and continued, "Remember, life is a battle-field of Kurukshetra where a psychological war of nerves and wits is being fought everyday. You have to be cleverer than your adversaries to survive in this evil world. The situation is quite hopeless and it may be too premature to predict the outcome, but I will certainly try to save you from the evil clutches of your opponents. At this late stage some unusual course may have to be adopted to expose the wicked game of these rascals." The problem was certainly grave but his stinging remarks were also to magnify the intensity of the fear in the mind of the client as his person and profession demanded.

Mr. Chawla thought for a few minutes, apparently pondering over the various issues of the case and the future course of action. He picked up the phone and dialed some number.

"Sardarji, *Sat Siri Akal*...How are you and how is everyone in the family? ... Yes...That...Of course, that was a great tragedy. But what can you do before the might of the Almighty ...Nothing special. I just wanted your help in a very genuine case. One of my friends will come to you tomorrow, if you are free, and explain to you every thing. Please do try to help him. He is an innocent person who has been wrongly implicated in a dirty case ...Oh! No, no...Not of that type... He is from Ludhiana. I will tell you all the details and the course of action later on ...O.K ... Yes ...Yes...Thank you. *Sat Siri Akal.*"

"I will give you the address of Mr. Chhabra. He lives in Kalupur. He is a Sikh gentleman and his forefathers have been living in Gujarat for decades. By virtue of his strong and assertive personality, he is the '*dada*' of the area and commands great respect. Meet him tomorrow and explain everything to him. I am sure he will be able to wriggle you out of this trap. By God's grace, everything will be all right." He reassured me and handed over a piece of paper to me with an address written on it.

I left the chamber of the lawyer with a mix of hope and despair, praying on the way that next day may prove to be auspicious. I had never had an encounter with a '*dada*', normally supposed to be a person of bad repute. What was in store for me? What if he refuses to help me? What will happen to my family if the case is decided against me? Engulfed in the midst of such fearful thoughts and feelings, I had no other option except to pray for some divine intervention and left everything to my destiny.

Next day, I was with Mr. Chhabra at the appointed time in the evening. He was apparently a fine Sikh gentleman in mid-fifties with partly grey beard and very strong muscular body. Little terrified, I introduced myself and greeted him with folded hands.

"*Sat Siri Akal.*"

"I think Chawlaji has sent you to me."

"Yes. He told me to meet you for my personal problem."

"Please sit down. Tell me complete details of the case."

"I will tell you the whole truth and shall not conceal anything."

I hesitated for a moment and looked at another man sitting there. Sardarji immediately understood the cause of my anxiety.

"Don't worry. He is Jaswinder, my younger son."

I greeted him also and told the complete truth to my benefactor. From his reactions, I could judge that he was getting convinced of my story. Regional and linguistic fraternity also came to my assistance in putting some more moral pressure on my expected saviour. As soon as I finished, he reflected for a few moments and turned towards his son.

"Jaswinder, go and call Bashir from his house...But remember, don't tell him anything. Just tell him that I have called him."

To me, he warned, "Be careful. Don't look at the man and pose as if you are not concerned with him." I nodded my head in confirmation of having received his instructions.

Jaswinder, a young man in his early twenties, was as strong and muscular as his father. Constantly looking at me, he had been patiently listening with his chin firmly dug in the palm of his left hand. He left only to come back after about five minutes.

"*Darji*, Bashir is not at home. He has gone to the market and may come back any time."

"You should have left a word with his wife."

"Yes, I have told her to send him as soon as he comes back from the market."

Anxious moments began to creep slowly and I impatiently awaited the arrival of the stranger. The past developments of the case quickly flashed before my eyes and I cursed myself for landing in such an ugly and shameful situation. I was not aware of what was in store for me. Who was this Bashir? Why had he been called? What is Sardarji going to ask him? Sound of every footstep would startle me as if Bashir had come. At last a tall bony fellow, wearing long shirt and '*salwar*', was in front of us. I could judge from the reaction on the face of Sardarji that he was Bashir.

Unaware of the impending hostile reception that lay ahead, he greeted Sardarji and said, "*Ustadji*, have you called me?"

Not revealing his inner intention, Sardarji said, "Yes Bashir, I have not seen you for the last many days. How is every one in the family?"

"Every thing is fine by the grace of Allah. What service can I do for you, *Ustadji*?"

"Nothing special. I just wanted to know, do you know this gentleman?" said Sardarji very innocently while pointing towards me.

Bashir looked at me carefully from top to bottom and then at Sardarji. I waited with bated breath for his reply. He looked at me once again. "No, I have never met him," said Bashir simultaneously nodding his head.

"Are you sure?"

"Of course, I am very sure. I have never seen him before. You know one glance of a person and the photograph gets permanently imprinted on my mind."

Sardarji lost his temper, got up from his seat like lightening and gave a full-blooded slap on Bashir's face. He now took off his shoe and started beating him left and right and simultaneously hurled all the abuses available in Gujarati dictionary. His ruthless behaviour completely took me by surprise and shock. In fear of some problem I immediately got up from my chair and went aside. Bashir virtually fell down on the ground and tried hard to save himself. The might of the blows having weakened, the perplexed victim struggled to get to his feet slowly, gasped for breath, and said, "But *Ustadj*i, what wrong have I done? Tell me at least my fault. I am like your son and you have never treated me like this."

"If you do not know this man then why are you putting him in trouble?"

"I really do not understand anything. How am I concerned with this man? How am I putting him in trouble when I even do not know him?"

"Sit down. I will tell you what grave wrong you are going to do to this gentleman." Sardarji pulled him closer, affectionately put his arm around his neck and ordered some water for him and tea for all. Apparently, he was trying to console Bashir and also giving him some time to recover from the shock.

"Are you going to the court next Friday to be a witness in some case?"

Bashir thought for a moment, trying to put some pressure on his mind to remember and said, "Yes, but what has that to do with your anger and brutal beating?"

"That is exactly what I am trying to tell you."

"*Ustadji,* I am not able to make head or tail of what you are saying. I request you not to ask riddles and tell me the fact."

"I will explain every thing to satisfy you. This Friday you are appearing in the court as a witness to give evidence that one Prem Makwana and his newly wedded wife had taken a room in your house on rent. One evening, you heard some loud argument in the room and by the time you came out, you saw two persons forcing Prem's wife into a three-wheeler and on his return you reported the matter to Prembhai."

The revelations were shocking and every word of Sardarji made Bashir's face more and more pale. He was perhaps unable to understand as to how Sardarji was aware of all this concoction.

"Is it true or not?"

"Yes, it is true," said Bashir with no other option with him except to confess the truth. "But *Ustadji*, how do you know all this?"

"Don't worry about this. You know my sources. He is the man against whom you are going to give evidence. Now tell me, did Prembhai ever stay in your house? Did you ever see this gentleman in or around your house?"

"*Ustadji*, please forgive me. Now I realise why you were so furious with me. I have always been seeking your advice on all such matters. This time only I did not ask you. Please pardon me."

"Yes, because now you consider yourself a super *'dada'*. I will forgive you if you tell me how much money you have taken for this false evidence?"

"I will not hide any thing from you. I took two hundred rupees and a bottle of rum from a friend of Prembhai. However, I promise that I will not go to the court now." He fell down on the feet of Sardarji with folded hands.

"You do not know what grave harm you would have done by giving false evidence against this man who has nothing to do with any case." Saying this, Sardarji immediately opened his cash box, took out some money and continued, "Here are five hundred rupees. Return the money and the rum bottle to the person. But do it only after Friday." After a few moments, he resumed, "And listen, do not talk to anyone and must appear in the court."

"I will do that. But tell me, how is my appearance going to help this man?"

"If you do not appear, Prembhai will try to produce some other false witness next time. You have to appear in the court as a hostile witness. Tell the truth that no one by the name Prem Makwana ever took a room in your house and that you do not know this gentleman. Do not change your stand even in the face of rigorous cross-examination. Also remember, I will be myself present in the court and if you try to play some mischief you know what all I can do."

"Do you think I can ever defy your orders? I will certainly do as directed by you."

"Don't say all this under pressure. Say, because it is the truth. You have to do this as a true Muslim. You are answerable to Allah."

"*Ustadji*, if you don't mind, may I know one thing from this man?"

"Yes, ask him any thing. He will tell you the truth."

"How has the girl been forcibly taken away and restored to her parents?"

Chhabra immediately intervened. "He has told me the whole truth. I will tell you later on. I can assure you, he has absolutely no role in this drama. The case may carry on for reconciliation or divorce but I am only concerned with your false evidence against this gentle soul. I am trying to save an innocent person. Let me also tell you, I do not know him and have no relation with him. Truth is the bond between us."

Bashir touched the feet of his *Ustad* with great reverence, stood up with folded hands and said, "*Ustadji,* I want to make one more request. Please do not put me to shame. Take this money back. I have done so many bad deeds in my life. Let me do one good one at least."

"Ok. Consider this not for what you have received from the other party. *Id* is round the corner. Let it be advance *Idi* for your children and wife. Now go. It is time for your *Namaz. Allah Hafiz.*"

Sardarji waited for a few moments, stood up and gave him a tight affectionate hug. Bashir was forcing back his tears and trying hard to conceal his emotions in my presence. He immediately turned back and left the place with the money softly clutched in his hands. Before leaving, Bashir looked at me and his silent gesture reassured me of his support.

I sat absolutely stunned and completely speechless while the entire shocking drama was being enacted. The incredible and nerve wrecking life experience appeared to be a scene from an action movie with no possibility of a retake. The key question that baffled me was how did Sardarji know that Bashir was the next witness? Probably, my lawyer had gathered the whole information and conveyed the same to Sardarji. I was, however, mighty thrilled and relieved at the favourable outcome of the whole episode and heaved a silent sigh of relief.

"Chawlaji had told me some details of the case and the rest I had guessed from my long experience with police and courts. It is just a coincidence that Bashir was the next witness. Though I could have tackled any other rogue also, it was easier for Bashir is my '*chela*' and is very sincere to me. I am happy that the man confessed the truth immediately. We have many more options to force such people to vomit out the truth, but it is always advisable to take out a thorn embedded in the flesh with a needle rather than with a sword," said Sardarji with a sense of arrogance and pride. After a little pause he continued, "I had to resort to such a seemingly reckless course, which is very mild in our business, for that was most effective under the circumstances. The situation was delicate and I did not want to give him any time to think of any excuse. Mean means have to be adopted sometimes even for a noble cause. You might have never come across such incidents in life before. It is routine with us. Now, don't worry at all and sleep peacefully. I will myself come to the court on Friday and keep a watch on Bashir. You never know these unscrupulous devils. They sell their conscience even for a paltry sum of money. But he is very much beholden to me and cannot repay my debt even in seven lives. He will not succumb to any pressure in my presence."

I looked at Sardarji with utmost satisfaction, folded my hands, and said, "I am extremely grateful to you and shall always remain deeply indebted to you throughout my life."

"Don't say all this. Impressed by your simplicity and impelled by my conscience I was convinced that you had helped your colleague with good intentions but had been falsely dragged in the case. Man is not bad, his times are sometimes bad. I also belong to Ludhiana and felt an inner urge to help you. But remember, never indulge in such matters. You seem to have no experience of courts and police. In these courts, nobody bothers about truth. What triumphs is the relative truth based on the version of the witnesses. Witnesses are bought and sold every moment and innocent people are hanged because of them. I confess that I myself have been quite a bad character but I have always tried that truth should not be defeated. I have left everything now and am running my honest business. It is after many years that the animal in me got wild and I decided to hit this man. Having lived with these people, I knew this tried and tested method would be most effective and a delay could have given him a chance to go in hiding and resurface only at the exact time of hearing. I am glad everything happened as per my plan and I have been of some use to you."

There are moments in life when words fail you. I was placed in such a situation. Sardarji waited for a while and continued, "I tell you, there is no court where I have not gone. There is no police station which I have not witnessed. The whole of this system is based on falsehood. Horse-trading goes on in these courts as in the field of politics. An honest person gets crucified at the altar of the blindfolded goddess of justice. Remember again, don't be so simple. Think of the consequences. Helping others is an irresistible virtue of the noble, but should not be at the cost of your own life. Imagine if Bashir had also given evidence against you, you would have been convicted of shameful charges. This would have resulted not only in the loss of your job and years of imprisonment but would have also given a tragic blow to your prestige and that of your family."

I trembled from top to bottom at the very imagination of such a situation. "You are right Sardarji. Innocent people suffer gravely at the hands of such a system. I would have been completely ruined but for you." I again expressed my deep gratitude and left satisfied hoping my woes to end next Friday.

Before leaving, Sardarji took me aside and warned, "You must exercise great caution. Do not disclose the facts of our meeting to any one even after the case is settled. It is like a war and you cannot afford to reveal your plans to your adversary. You are a highly educated person but remember, winners don't reveal their strategy to others. Difference between winning and losing is one right move, and one wrong move may frustrate all the hard work done. Let it remain a complete enigma forever. Your profession does not teach you all these realities of life but try to learn the way the world actually goes."

Realising the importance of his advice, I completely sealed my lips and did not talk to anyone about the meeting. I took care not to talk to even my wife till Friday. I managed to retain the normal sense of fear on my face and continued to display usual worry in my behaviour.

Finally the eagerly awaited Friday arrived. All of us reached the court before time. Bashir and Prem Makwana were spotted together. They were talking quite freely. Prem seemed to be busy reassuring Bashir about our identity lest he should make a mistake at the eleventh hour in recognising us. True to his promise, Sardarji was there well in time. With the call, all of us entered the court-room. Bashir was called in the witness box.

"Your name?" asked Prembhai's lawyer.

"Sir, my name is Bashir Ahmed."

"Where are you living?"

"Sir, I am living in Kalupur."

"Are you living in your own house or in a rented house?"

"It is my own house, sir."

"Did you ever give a room of your house on rent to one Mr. Prembhai Makwana?"

Bashir posed little outward surprise and then replied, "Sir, I have never given my house or a part of it on rent to anyone so far."

The lawyer was completely stunned at the unexpected reply of Bashir. He thought that the witness had erred in understanding the question and repeated the same. Unable to get the desired reply, he reframed his question in various different ways and made more unsuccessful attempts in the hope of getting the expected and tutored reply from the carefully cooked witness. He was utterly shocked at the dramatic shift in the planned strategy. In spite of his best efforts, Bashir could not be intimidated into abandoning or contracting his testimony. Being an experienced witness who had appeared in courts several times, he withstood the prolonged grilling during cross-examination with perfect ease and did not crumble under sustained pressure. His firmness had put the lawyer in an extremely hapless situation. The lawyer nervously looked at Bashir, glanced at the judge and others present in the room. Thoroughly embarrassed, he pulled out his handkerchief from his pocket, wiped the visible drops of perspiration from his forehead and had no other option but to resume his seat.

The evidence of Bashir finally clinched the whole issue and brought a wave of immense joy and satisfaction to all of us. Perhaps the most satisfied persons were Sardarji and my lawyer. Tears of joy were suspended on the fringes of the eyes of my wife. My saviour got up and immediately left the court. He made sure not to look at me to give even an iota of hint to anyone about our relations. The fate of the case was finally sealed and had completely shifted in my favour in the span of five minutes. Bashir was seen surrounded by Prembhai and his accomplices who had pinned high hopes on him. From their reactions and gestures, it was evident that they were accusing him of betraying the faith reposed in him. They were completely bewildered at the turn of the events and Bashir's U-turn had come to them as a bombshell. They were crestfallen and it was as if a mountain of doom and gloom had descended on them. Their hopes had virtually collapsed like a house of cards and they had no option but to resign themselves to their fate. Bashir looked at me from the corner of his eye and I smiled in gratitude. On my part, I displayed a great feeling of surprise and ignorance mingled with happiness on my face. Lalwanis had never dreamt of such an unexpected and dramatic twist in the case. They asked me about the surprised turn of events but the closely guarded secret was not revealed to them by me and it remained a mystery ever after. I waited there for sometime more to let the feeling of joy completely sink in me and then left the court with my wife.

The conclusive testimony of Bashir had miraculously altered the course of the case against me. The charges were finally dropped. The post mortem of the case fully vindicated my faith in the strength of our judicial system. It reinforced my conviction that truth always triumphs finally and that it is not subservient to the whims and fancies of the cheats. Our disillusionment with our judicial system is sometimes due to our lack of patience. Justice, howsoever delayed, is not denied. It was also amply evident that witnesses are not always sold or bought. Both Chhabra and Bashir had played a critical role in the case and this left a deep imprint on my mind. I always held them with immense reverence and veneration for boldly standing by the truth. In return, they only gracefully accepted my heartfelt thanks. I lost track of further developments since I was transferred from Ahmedabad on the completion of my tenure. I heard later on that the divorce suit was filed and the same was granted by the court. In reality, I had great sympathy for sincere lovers like Prembhai whose love is crucified by the prejudices of the society and hatred of Lalwanis. Prembhai and Veena fell in love but, unfortunately, could not stay in love. Their relations crumbled under the social pressure of caste and status. In course of time the whole episode was confined to the backwaters of my memory and the case was obscured in the midst of time. However, I have always been haunted by the fact that the dreams and aspirations of many a young lover are crucified at the cruel hands of social, economic, caste, creed, community and religious barriers. Let us hope for the day when sincere and true love-birds shall be free from such pernicious captivities and shall be free to enjoy their desired course of love.

❐

8
A Lost Pilgrim

She was hardly ten years old and was studying in the fifth grade in a village primary school. The school was about three kilometres from her village and she had to get up very early in the morning with the crowing of the cock, and prepare lunch for her father and herself before leaving for the school. By nature, she was a lover of cleanliness. She would daily broom her cottage and surrounding areas. Inside and outside of the hut was plastered with mud and cow dung every week. Walls inside the hut were decorated by her with some paintings of gods and goddesses. She was deprived of the love and care of her mother who had left her when she was only five years old. She was brought up by her father, Khusia, who was a farm-labourer earning pittance wages of about one hundred rupees a day. These wages were also not regular as they depended on the sowing or harvesting days only. Other days were spent in collecting fire wood from the thick forest full of wild animals and selling the same in the nearby town. Life was treacherous for the poor family and only they could feel the pangs of poverty. Their only abode was a broken hut with thatched roof that was more like a sieve showing moonlight at night. During rains, it was difficult to find some dry corner and nights were spent with drenched clothes that dried next day courtesy wind and sunshine. Basic necessities of life were out of question, but there was still happiness and satisfaction in life. Kali, born on a pitch-dark night as her name meant, was determined to provide all possible comforts and joy to her father and also to continue her education.

Kali was an extremely affectionate little girl loved by all the village folk. She was hardworking, sweet by nature and intelligent by her age. Dark in complexion with sparklingly white teeth, chiseled features and long jet black hair, she was charming as per the standards of beauty of her society. Even with meager possessions, both father and daughter were blessed with divine virtue of sharing and were ever ready to help others in distress. She would not hesitate to part with her little firewood when demanded by any needy neighbour. She would always ensure that their hearth was kept burning during rains even if she had to tie a wet cloth on her small belly to suppress her hunger. She always sought her happiness in the joy of others. Villagers on their part were also helpful to her because of her generosity. Her father was equally kind and the motherless girl had imbibed all these qualities of heart from her parents.

One day, while running to her school for the fear of any punishment of being late, she suddenly heard someone moaning in the deserted jungle through which she had to pass on way to her school. Initially she did not take notice but suddenly turned back and saw a man lying behind her. She immediately retraced her steps forgetting the punishment on account of her late arrival in the school. She put her bag on the ground, turned the man who was lying on his stomach. An old man, frail in body with no visible strength, completely drenched in sweat was before her. She hesitatingly touched her and felt signs of life, even though he was absolutely motionless. She looked around to see for some help but all in vain. No one was visible. Kali took out her little dusty plastic bottle of water to pour a few drops in the mouth of the old man. She could hardly force open his mouth, but some drops did slide in. There was no visible movement. A few drops more and the man moved his hands and eyes a bit. There was glimmer of a tiny ray of hope on her face. She was delighted and tears of joy spattered in her sparkling eyes. She helped the man sit against a tree trunk and gave him some more water. The man opened his eyes, looked around in bewilderment and again closed them. She was happy that the old man was alive. She asked him about his health and whereabouts but the man simply looked at her as if he had not understood anything. In the tense situation of nursing the stranger, she completely forgot about her school. Fortunately for her, two men came that way and with their help she brought the old man to her hut.

Khusia had gone for his labour-job at that time and there was none in the hut. She warmed the mushy meal that she had taken for her lunch and served the same to the old man. Kali tried to feed him with her tiny soft hands but the man was too feeble to chew the stone-hard *chapatti*. He could hardly swallow a few morsels. Too weak to sit, he again dropped dead on the sagging cot. Kali tried to talk to him but the man did not utter even a single word and it appeared from his reactions that he had not understood anything. In the evening, Khusia also tried but the old man had no strength to even open his lips. With folded hands Kali prayed to God for the recovery of the stranger. In abject poverty, when even two square meals were rare, milk was a luxury and not seen by Kali for months. She still managed to borrow half a cup from someone for the old man. This gave him some strength and he was fresh and slightly better in the morning. In utter astonishment he looked at the queer surroundings, but greeted the little girl with a warm smile. No one realised at that time that small moments create history and no act of kindness, howsoever small, is ever wasted.

Efforts started again in the morning to know the name and whereabouts of the stranger but all proved futile. He would only point to himself and then to a direction perhaps indicating that he was from 'that' place. He spoke some incoherent words not understood by anyone. Regarding his name he said 'Murugan' which people interpreted as 'Muru Gram'. They thought it to be the name of some village, but none could recollect having ever heard such a name. Rumour of the presence of a stranger in Kali's hut spread faster than light and the 'stranger' soon changed into 'alien'. Men, women and children flocked to Kali's hut to have a glimpse of the 'alien', but soon realised that he was not an alien but a man from their own world. Children smiled, laughed and made humiliating gestures. Some ridiculed him and made fun of the old man. Kali was very furious at them and threatened to hit them if they mocked at her 'Mushi Baba' as she fondly began to address him because of his thick moustache. She would stroke his moustache with her tiny little fingers and the old man would enjoy her childish pranks. Sometimes he would deliberately hold her hand to touch his moustache, smile and then both would burst into full blooded waves of joyful laughter. Kali was distressed since her Mushi Baba was not able to express himself because of the language problem as his senses of hearing and speaking were perfect. Smiles, eyes, and hand gestures were the only convenient modes of communication and both had soon mastered the art.

The problem of locating Mushy Baba's home and restoring him to his relatives was the talk of all village-folk.

Baba sometimes uttered 'idli' which suggested that he was a Madrasi as all south Indians were called in that area. An idea accidently popped up in the mind of a sensible person. He suggested that many trucks rest at the *dhaba* on the highway and some south Indian driver may be able to help them in understanding the language of the poor man. It was decided to take him to the *dhaba* at night, but he refused to go without Kali. Though there was no apparent reason, an unfounded fear was always in the eyes of Murugan. He would go out only by holding her hand as if he was safer in the custody of the small little girl than with a strong man. He clearly gestured that Kali must accompany him. Finally, it was decided that both Kali and her father should also go with Mushi Baba to the *dhaba* to solve the mystery of the whereabouts of the old man who had been away from his home for over a week now. Unfortunately no truck driver from the south came on that night. The effort was repeated next night also, but all in vain. Finally, on the third night a truck driver from the south came. Kali immediately ran to him and told him non-stop the problem that she was facing. She brought the driver to Mushi Baba and the discussion in their language started. Kali clapped violently in merriment at the success of her effort and was keenly listening to the discussion between the two persons though she could not make even head or tail of the gist. There were ripples of joy on her face as her Mushi Baba was very happy and was joyfully looking at Kali and often pointing to her during the course of discussion.

The truck driver told Khusia that the old man's name was Murugan and he was from a remote small village in Trichi district of Tamil Nadu. Murugan did not recollect any phone number and refused to go with the driver as he was too terrified to go with any person except with some known person from his village. The driver told them that he would contact someone from that or the nearby village and arrange to bring some friend of Murugan. Strangely, throughout the discussion the old man kept on holding the finger of Kali tightly for the fear of being taken away by the driver even though he was from his own area. Thankfully, the mystery was solved to some extent and the driver promised to come back soon with some friend of Murugan. Kali profusely thanked the driver and past midnight all returned home satisfied at the success of their effort. Little Kali was the happiest person as if she had successfully located a treasure. Mushi Baba held her in her lap, hugged her and kissed her for the first time. Kali in her innocence repeated the gesture and refused to come down from the lap of her Mushi Baba.

Smiles of satisfaction returned to the lives of both Murugan and Kali. Meaning of life and depth of love had changed for Murugan. He started following a routine. He would get up in the morning, say his prayers and then go with Khusia to the farm or with Kali to her school. First he thought that Khusia had his own land but soon realised that he was a labourer on someone's farm. He offered to work with him but Khusia would hold his shoulders and make him sit under the shade of the tree while he was busy in his labour work. Mushi Baba often went with Kali to her school. He would sit there and accompany her back to the hut. They conversed more easily now in the language of smiles and gestures and it appeared as if both fully understood each other. One day Kali took Mushi baba to the place from where she had first picked him and pointed to the spot. Mushi Baba did not remember anything and paid no heed to the actions of Kali. She realised that he did not remember anything.

In happiness, the days started passing very quickly. After about a fortnight, a taxi was seen on the dusty road of the village. Two persons were seated in that and one would often come out and inquire something from the village folk. Finally, a villager brought them to Kali's hut and the two men came to the bamboo door of the thatched hut. One of them immediately ran inside, hugged Murugan and started talking to him in their language. Kali was first shocked at the sudden appearance of the two strangers but soon realised that the truck driver must have sent the persons from the village of Mushi Baba. Murugan pointed to Kali, said something and one of them blessed her by placing his hand on her head. Kali could understand that Mushi Baba was introducing her to his friends. Khusia also came running from the farm on hearing the arrival of the car and the two strangers. With some difficulty, he arranged to prepare some tea for all. Some villagers also gathered and were getting convinced that Murugan must be a wealthy man as his friends had come to the village in a taxi.

Murugan and his friends wanted to leave the same evening but Kali held Mushi Baba's hand and with tears in her eyes gestured him 'no', pulled his hand and forced him to sit down. Murugan was also moved by the love of Kali. Curious is the dynamics of love, which reason cannot explain. It is not slave of social, cultural or geographical affinity. Love of strangers is sometimes stronger while blood relations become sworn enemies. Blood relations often demand something in return for their love but love of strangers may be selfless and undemanding. Some relations have no relevance or name, but are stronger than any relation. Such was her relation with her Baba. Love's relation with time is also an enigma. In love, time runs faster, but strangulates and hardly creeps in distress. Moments of joy and love are short while those of separation are long. Love is both strength and weakness, but for the small child, love for her mentor became her weakness.

Murugan did not want to leave Kali but destiny had willed it otherwise. He had to go. All these days, Kali was beyond herself with joy, had started paying more attention to her studies, besides looking after all the comforts of her Mushi Baba. She never imagined that day of separation would also come though she wanted Murugan to go back and join his family. The innocent girl failed to realise that her Mushi Baba could not be both with her and his family. At night, she could not sleep and kept on weeping, crying and murmuring something during sleep. She began to fear that intensity of love would decrease with distance and Mushi Baba would soon forget her. Love was leaving both on the crossroad of life. Murugan realised that Kali was sad due to separation and could not bear his leaving her. It is true; greater the love more is the pain of separation.

The tragic tale of Murugan's misery was unfolded by the friends who were with him when he was lost somewhere during their pilgrimage. Three friends from the same village, all devout worshippers of Lord Shiva, decided to visit Puri to participate in the Rath Yatra of Lord Jagan Nath. While the two were little educated and could converse in some scratchy Hindi, Murugan did not know any language except Tamil. During such pilgrimages thousands of devotees lose their lives in a bid to have an early and clear glimpse of their God. The old, women and children become easy victims of stampedes. Repeated warnings and good arrangements also fail and the tragedy is repeated every year at various places all over the world. No lessons are learnt in spite of grave human losses and they are soon forgotten to be repeated again and again. Murugan also became a victim of one such stampede. Fortunately, he was on the edge of the crowd and was not crushed after his fall. Some strong man immediately pushed him aside and left him unconscious on the side of the road. His friends had moved ahead and Murugan was lost in his bid to pay homage to the Lord.

The tragedy did not end here. All efforts by his two associates to trace Murugan failed and the two returned home without their friend hoping for his arrival in the village. As he regained consciousness, he tried to seek help from someone but the problem of language came as a strong barrier. Two persons offered to help him but turned out to be thieves. They robbed him of his money and the gold chain that he normally wore and on the pretext of taking him to his home, left him in the jungle at the mercy of wild animals and vagaries of nature. It was here that he lay hungry and thirsty for two days and did not remember anything afterwards. On regaining consciousness, he was in a thatched hut in a village with a small little girl nursing him by his side.

Life is a chain of unexpected events. The day of departure and separation came. Murugan could see tears of sadness suspended in the bright shining eyes of the little affectionate baby. He wanted to spend some more time with her and took her and her father to the nearby town in the taxi. Kali was thrilled, though fear of ultimate separation was always haunting her. She remained silent throughout the journey, holding the hand of Baba. Murugan tried to break her sadness by placing her little fingers on his moustache. She did smile, but soon dropped her chin. All the time she was resting her head on his shoulder as if to say "Please do not leave me."

Murugan bought a pair of good dresses for her and two sets of *kurta* and *dhoti* for Khusia. He bought a mobile phone for Khusia and got a sim card also in his name. Friend of Murugan explained to Kali, "This is not a very costly phone. He will buy a good phone for you when you grow. He will talk to you on the phone and soon pay a visit. He will let you know about the programme."

"But how will Baba talk to me in Hindi?" asked the curious girl.

"I will explain to you everything that he would like to convey to you." Still Kali learnt a few Tamil words and wrote them in Hindi in her notebook. She decided to learn Tamil to frequently and freely talk directly to Mushi Baba.

After reaching home, all had a final cup of tea and Murugan departed with a solemn promise to return soon to meet his sweet baby. Kali waved with her loving eyes overflowing with tears. Mushi Baba responded with a fake faint smile and tears of separation in his eyes.

Pain of separation is universally inevitable and only the sufferers can realise its pang. It can only be felt and not described in words. Separation is also the promise and hope of a new life. Though sad, Kali was optimistic to soon meet Mushi Baba. With his departure she suddenly became more sober and preferred to remain silent. From a naughty, chirpy little village girl, she was transformed into a silence-loving serious girl. She hardly talked to other village girls on her firewood collection errands and even with her father. It was difficult to fathom the depth of her grief. She would often keep on sitting on the door of her hut looking in one direction as if she was waiting for someone. Her condition was like a drop of water hidden in a lonely cloud, not knowing whether it would fall on a parched piece of land and vanish or in a sea-shell to become a pearl. Lonely in the path of life, even jokes refused to bring any joy to her face. Food lost all taste and she would never feel hungry. Concentration on studies also became less though she did not neglect them as directed by her Baba. Sitting alone, she was always dreaming of her Mushi Baba with eyes wide open. Looking in vacant spaces, she would sometimes smile and again become sad. Her usual smile had completely withered from her comely lips and she would bury her head in her hands and sob silently. She would murmur some inaudible words in her deep slumber. She was learning to live with pain of separation rather than display it, but the emotional quotient of pain of separation was very high in the sweet sensitive girl. She wondered when the harrowing time of separation will come to an end. She was so desperate to talk to Baba that everyday she would enquire from her father if there was a call. At night also, she was frequently startled by the slight noise outside expecting Mushi Baba knocking at the door. She sometimes dreamt that she is playing in a garden blossoming with flowers when her Mushi Baba comes to her from nowhere, embraces her, holds her in his lap and tells her, "I am here. I will stay here. I will never go back again." She would also wear the new dress in the vain hope of Baba's arrival and would stand at the door of her hut for hours looking in the direction from which the car had arrived. Human heart is a source of infinite desires but her only desire was to have wings and fly to her dear Baba and cling to him forever.

Four days after the departure of Murugan, the phone bell rang in the evening. Kali immediately told her father, "This is Baba. This is Baba's call." She was over the moon with joy. Murugan had called her.

"Kali!" She recognised the voice of her Baba.

"Appa. Alo. Vanakkam." She immediately spoke the three words of Tamil which she had mastered and rehearsed.

Murugan was completely surprised but extremely pleased. He answered in Tamil, but Kali could not understand anything as her vocabulary of Tamil was limited to only half-a-dozen common words.

"Kali, your Murugan uncle is here with me. He is absolutely surprised but thrilled at your speaking Tamil. He wants you to learn little more. Next time, I will bring a book for you. He wants to know about your welfare. He says that you should not be sad. He will come next month to meet you all. He wants that you must concentrate on your studies as that was most important in life."

"Please tell Baba I am all right, though little sad. But now, I am happy after receiving his call. Why did you take so many days to give us a call? I have been impatiently expecting it everyday. Please tell him that I am going to school regularly and studying hard. He should not worry. Tell him to come soon. I miss him very much." She also wanted him to see the new dress that she was wearing, not realising in her innocence that Mushi Baba was not able to see her dress on the phone. She could not control herself and started crying.

"Kali!"

"Appa, naan unnai virumpukiren. Pittu vareni."

Murugan also responded in Tamil saying, "I love you. Good bye."

"Miga nandri, Appa."

Murugan was beyond himself with joy on conversing in Tamil with his loving daughter and gave her a call almost everyday. Time now began to pass very quickly for both. One day, she received a call that her Mushi Baba would be coming next Sunday. She wore her new dress, combed her hair properly and looked into the palm-sized piece of broken mirror hung on the broken wall of the hut. She was ready early in the morning anxiously waiting for the arrival of the car of her Baba. Time stagnates in anxious moments of wait. Finally, the uncertainty passed and the much-awaited moment arrived. She spotted the car and madly ran towards it in a bid to stop it. Fortunately, bump into the car was avoided. There were ripples of joy on her face and her eyes were lit up with delight. She clung to Baba, started crying loudly and refused to leave him even on the persistent requests of her father. Having exhausted the quota of her tears, she brought him and his friend to the hut. She had specially cleaned the hut on that day, decorated it with some wild flowers and had spread on the cot a washed bed sheet crudely repaired with patches of coloured cloth. She rubbed her eyes in disbelief and pinched her arm to make sure that it was not a dream. She sat with Baba, holding his hand and putting her head on his lap. She again stroked his moustache with her fingers and both had a very loud hearty laugh. Their bond of unconditional mutual love was unique and had no parallels.

This time, Murugan had come with his childhood friend Kumaran to help him bargain and buy a piece of about three acres of agriculture land in that or in any nearby village. Murugan had earlier revealed to his friend that one night, he heard rumbling stomach of both father and daughter and realised that both had slept hungry even though they had arranged food for him. He was overwhelmed by the sacrifice of both for a stranger and it was at that defining moment that he decided to adopt Kali as his daughter and do everything for them in life. Fortunately, they could get a good piece of fertile land in a nearby village. A high school was also only two kilometres away. Kali's father was surprised at this bargain and wondered why Murugan was buying land in their area. On arrival back to the hut, Kumaran told Khusia the purpose of buying the land.

"Murugan has decided to buy this land for you," said Kumaran.

Khusia was completely taken aback and questioned, "Why for us?"

"This is his wish. Actually, the land is not in your name. It is in the name of Kali. You will work on this land and produce food grain, which should be sufficient for your livelihood and for the education of Kali."

"But we cannot accept this," said Khusia emphatically.

"You cannot say no. Murugan is gifting it to his daughter. He will also deposit some money in her account tomorrow in the nearby bank."

Khusia stood up with folded hands and holding hands of Murugan said in a discrete way of saying 'no', "Please do not do this. We are poor people but fully satisfied with our lot. God has given me such a lovely and dutiful daughter and I have nothing more to ask Him. I earnestly request you not to load us with this burden. I will not be able to repay in ten lives."

Kali was completely amazed and sat speechless. She kept on looking at Baba, his friend and her father and could not understand anything. Finally, she also got up and told Baba by nodding her head in negative. In her rustic innocence she pleaded, "We do not want all this. All I want are your blessings. I want your love. I only want you to keep visiting us occasionally. I will work hard for my father and we will earn but we cannot take this."

Mushi Baba pulled Kali closer to him, lovingly stroked her cheek and put his finger on her lips indicating her to keep quiet.

Kumaran told Kali, “He says daughters cannot refuse gifts from their fathers. It is their right.”

He also says, “I have enough by God’s grace and being a bachelor have no children or anyone to inherit my huge farming land in Tamil Nadu. What I am giving is nothing. This is just the beginning. Grow up and then we will discuss more about this.”

He also says, “Kali’s care and love for me was selfless. She sacrificed everything for me. She remained hungry to ensure my survival. She remained thirsty to quench my thirst. She slept on the floor to see that I was comfortable. She made me happy knowing that I was a stranger and will leave her one day. She is not only my daughter, but also goddess for me as she has given me a new birth. I am alive today only because of her. She is my very being. I love her as I love my god. I cannot repay even if I give her everything that I have.”

He is telling me to tell you clearly, “This ends the topic. I am fiercely determined and will entertain no more discussion on this. He will give you money to build a small *pucca* house on this land and to live there. Kali’s high school is also close to the land. She must continue her studies. As she grows her future will be decided by him in consultation with Khusia. Let me also tell you that he is undeterred in his resolve and will not deviate from his decision.”

Kumaran told Kali that her Baba wants her to warm the food brought from the market and serve to all. He is feeling very hungry. With this, Murugan gestured to Kali by putting his fingers on his mouth and his hand on his stomach.

Kumaran said, “Kali, he is saying that let us all sit together and eat. The family that eats together, stays together.” Kali could not say anything and immediately got up to obey the command of her godfather.

Murugan stayed with Kali for a week. During this period, he bought three acres of farmland in the name of Kali, arranged construction of a small house on this land and opened a savings account in a bank in the name of Kali. After having finished his decided work, he left promising to pay frequent visits to monitor the progress of work on the farmland, construction of the house and education of Kali. He was very particular about her education and always advised her to work hard in studies and do not discontinue them.

Days passed into months and months into years. Kali was now a grown-up girl. She had passed her tenth class examination with exceptionally good score. Khusia's regular work on his small piece of land had helped him save some money for the marriage of his daughter. Murugan had also been regularly depositing some money in her account and had been looking after all her physical and financial needs during his visits. He now wanted Khusia to find a suitable match for Kali. Khusia left this responsibility to her godfather. Years had brought Kali emotionally closer to her Mushi Baba, though she was now more reserved and not as chirpy as before. Their discussions were now on more serious social issues and Murugan was happy at the all-round development and maturity of his daughter. With his determination, Murugan learnt some Hindi from Kali proving that if one aspires, age is just a number. To talk directly and more frequently, Kali had picked up some working vocabulary of Tamil. Mutual conversations now became an everyday affair as the language barriers had been completely demolished.

On one of the visits, warm and benevolent Murugan opened the topic of marriage with Kali to know her reaction. "Kali my child, I want you to now settle down in life and look after your old fathers. This is the ripe time for your marriage." Kali simply looked at the ground and did not say anything. She felt very shy to talk on such a sensitive topic concerning her.

"Should I find some suitable match for you?"

"What can I say? It is for you or papa to decide. I have nothing to say on this subject."

Murugan told Khusia that Kumaran who had been often coming there had great liking for Kali particularly due to her very affectionate nature and her habit of serving and looking after the elders. His son was B.Com. and was working in a bank in Trichi. Events developed at a very fast pace. Murugan wanted both Khusia and Kali to accompany him and see the boy and also the family. The boy had one elder sister who was married and well-settled. Kali also did not object to the suggestion and all the three went to Trichi with Murugan. The boy was liked by all but Murugan still wanted both Kali and Khusia to consider all aspects before taking the vital decision of marriage. He, however, assured them of the good and progressive nature of the boy whom he had watched closely since his childhood. It is said that marriages are arranged in heaven and performed on earth. The proposal was finally approved by both families and the prospective bride and groom. Life is full of glorious improbabilities. No one would have ever imagined Kali's coming to Tamil Nadu and marrying a Tamil boy. Murugan made all marriage arrangements as father of Kali. In course of time Khusia sold the farm land and came to stay with Murugan who was above sixty and had none to look after him. He also shifted to Trichy and both started living in an apartment in the society where Kali and her family were living. Kali was now a rich woman having inherited the property of her benevolent Mushi Baba.

Murugan had picked up good Hindi. Pointing to Kali's son, who was merrily enjoying the warmth of Baba's lap, he said, "Now I will be able to talk to him in Hindi also. We can go on a pilgrimage anywhere in India and I will not be lost." Kali looked at her Mushi Baba and simply blushed.

❐

9
When the Storm Comes Again

The bald-headed judge entered the court-room, resumed his seat and ordered the accused to be produced in the court. A frail, curly haired young fisher-woman, about twenty years old, was escorted inside the room by two police-women. She was wearing neat dress, a '*saree*' typical of the style worn by the women of her clan. Slightly darker in complexion, she was smart and charming in appearance. She had tresses of jet black hair properly tucked in a bun. Her cheerful disposition was unaware of the impending gloom that lay ahead. She bowed with folded hands and went straight to the witness box without any signal or order, for a few early appearances had made her fully conversant with the court courtesies. Glancing casually through his glasses, the judge said, "Mrs. Mary D'Souza, before I pronounce the judgement in your case, have you anything to say in your defence?"

"My lord, on the very first day, I had told the complete truth, for I have never told a lie in my life. I reiterate that I am innocent. I have not murdered my husband. I did push him into the shallow waters on the sea-shore, but never with the motive of killing him. I did quarrel with John a couple of times and also on that fateful evening. I swear I had never had the slightest intention of harming him for I intensely loved him. I wanted him to work like other fishermen and earn his livelihood. I am not guilty of committing any crime and am confident that your honour will do justice." Mary had no difficulty in reconstructing the sequence of events and said all this in one breath. There was a sense of perfect confidence and complete absence of any emotional nervousness or feeling of guilt in her statement. She believed that truth will triumph in the court of justice. Her age and innocence were completely ignorant of the working of the legal system and the heart-wrenching punishment that awaited her fate.

The stone-cold judge appeared to pay scant attention to Mary's long statement for it was sheer repetition of what she had stated on all her previous appearances. Having completed the formality of asking the accused for the last time, the learned judge adjusted his glasses, casually looked at Mary and pronounced the verdict.

"From the circumstances and the events that preceded the mysterious death of Mr. John D'Souza, it is abundantly evident that his wife, Mrs. Mary D'Souza, had strained relations with her husband and was always quarreling with him. She had also beaten him on many occasions in the presence of the village-folk. On the evening of 23rd September, she had threatened to throw him into the deep sea and was seen actually pushing him violently into the water amidst heavy downpour and unprecedented stormy weather. Her repeated assertion that she only pushed him into shallow water where, according to her, a man could not be drowned, is not acceptable. Whatever the cause of friction and confrontation between the two, her action proves beyond doubt her intention and deliberate attempt to kill her husband. Her coming back to the hut after pushing him into the sea and not caring to know his fate throughout the night further confirms her motive. Due to continued sea-storm the body of Mr. John D'Souza could not be traced and was later on seen floating in the sea by an eye witness. Mrs. Mary D'Souza's self-confession of having threatened to kill her husband, followed by physically pushing him into the sea, are sufficient proofs beyond doubt of her murderous intentions and of her having actually committed the crime. The chain of circumstantial evidence and testimony of the prime witness substantiate the charge of murder beyond any reasonable doubt. This not being a rarest of the rare cases, she does not deserve death sentence and is sentenced to life imprisonment."

Though on expected lines, the verdict was a terrible shock and shook her inner recesses. She was unaware of the magnitude of the problem and the grievous blow completely shattered her faint hope of release. The hushed silence all around was suddenly broken. "This is injustice...This is not fair...I did not kill him...I always loved him...I only wanted him to work like other men...." All her tears, wailings and entities failed to move the judge and her plea for mercy was not entertained. She completely broke down and fell on the railings of the witness-box. Her fate was a forgone conclusion though she did not expect her conviction due to her complete ignorance of the legal process. There was none to listen to her cries and repeated assertions of innocence. In spite of her imploring she was dragged out of the court-room by the police amidst the mixed reactions of the audience.

Some men from her village who had gathered to witness the last scene of the rare drama were happy at the judgment and were whispering, "She was very cruel to John. She is actually responsible for his death. She deserved this punishment." A few others were in a state of shock. They termed the judgment as shockingly unfair. They sympathised with the plight of the hapless woman and felt disillusioned at the fateful decision. They were sad, dejected and silent. They were convinced that there was lack of direct evidence and she had been convicted only on the basis of circumstantial evidence. The prime witness, who was supposed to have seen the dead body of John, was himself a person of dubious character and actually wanted to take revenge from Mary for she had once rejected his marriage proposal. In their opinion, the court mainly based the conviction on his statement and erred in judgment.

Escorted by the police, Mary left the court-room and boarded a waiting police van. On the way to the prison, just by a coincidence, she passed by the church where she had been married only last year during these very days. The ringing of the church bells violently echoed in her ears. She prayed for permission to visit the church and out of sheer compassion, the escorting police officer granted her the same. She ran straight to the Father to confess everything before him.

"Father, I told the complete truth in the court. I did not kill John whom I loved intensely and beyond words. I swear before the Lord, I did not kill him. I am innocent."

With a solemn expression on his face, Father consoled Mary and said, "Do not grieve, my child. Remember, path of love is thorny and not smooth and love sometimes leaves you alone on the cross road of life. In this lie-dominated society, truth may not succeed immediately but it will ultimately triumph in His court."

"When will that day come?" asked the innocent girl.

"Mysterious are the ways of God. He puts His beloved ones to test. Obey His command gladly and that will be the greatest service to the Lord. Pain is a part of life and everyone has to bear the share of his misfortunes. Do not lose your composure in adversity for real test of character is in distress. Remember, sunshine always follows darkness. Before reaching dawn, night has to pass through darkness. Never abandon the path of hope even though it is laden with thorns. I can see light for you at the end of the tunnel." Father blessed her by placing his hand on her head.

Mary's age and innocence could not understand this deep philosophy of life. Her searching eyes were busy finding a satisfactory reply to her question. With a faint smile on her cheeks, she continued, "Father, happiness did occasionally knock on my door but it generally betrayed me. I could never imagine that life could be so cruel. There is complete darkness all around now."

"Keep smiling my child, for misery lessens in the face of smile. Remember, ups and downs are a part of life. All pains shall slowly creep into the past. Darkness is only when you close your eyes. Open them and light will be all around."

"You know Father, I have never harmed anyone and have always loved others."

"I know you Mary. Continue to love everyone. It gives pleasure though it is painful too. Still, love is the nucleus of all existence. It is the essence of all creation. Be always happy. Happiness is like light, when it spreads it engulfs darkness within and without."

With a feeling of extreme distress discernable on her face and tears of repentance trickling down her dry cheeks, Mary knelt down and held Father by her hand. An old incident suddenly began to flash on the inward eye of the Father.

Fourteen years back an orphan girl, hardly five years old, was brought to the church by her maternal uncle for there was none to look after her. One day this little girl stole the frock of her friend. That evening Father assembled all children and said, "I have called you here, for Rosy has lost her new frock. She suspects that someone has stolen the same. You know stealing is a sin and God punishes those who take away the property of others. I want you to confess before me if anyone of you is responsible for the theft."

With her usual luminous innocence and without a moment's hesitation, Mary stepped forward, reverently bowed down and confessed, "Father, the frock is with me. Actually I did not take it with the intention of stealing it. I liked it and was tempted to wear it once at night and would have returned it to Rosy tomorrow." Mary said all this with no apparent feeling of guilt in her mind.

"It is good that you have confessed your mistake. Repentance is a great virtue. May the Lord pardon you. But, it would have been better if you had requested Rosy for the same."

"This is my mistake, Father. You may give me any punishment, but I promise, I will never do it again in future," said the innocent girl.

Father was visibly moved by her innocence and did not even think of awarding any punishment to Mary as he knew that tears of repentance were more effective than tears of punishment. "There is no greater punishment than the realisation of one's mistake. May God be always kind to you, my child."

Mary immediately ran to her room, brought the frock and thankfully handed it over to Rosy.

"Please forgive me Rosy. I thought you may not allow me to put on if I make a request to you," said the little girl while handing over the frock to its rightful owner.

Realising that the values of truth and honesty could be inculcated and strengthened by fulfilling the natural desires of the children, he said, “Rosy my child, now give the frock to Mary and let her wear it this evening.”

Father blessed the children and left. Mary stood there like a statue with her eyes chasing the footsteps of the Father. Tears of joy were waiting to role down her comely cheeks. Her tiny sparkling eyes reflected a sense of repentance and an inner determination.

Suddenly, there was violent dust storm and dark threatening clouds indicated onslaught of torrential rains. The sound of the deafening horn of the police van pierced the horrid quiet and Mary was startled. She struggled to get up with a heavy heart. Father blessed Mary and said, “Go my child. Confront the problems with courage and don’t run away from them. Facing the problem boldly lessens the pain. Time will decide the best for you. I am fully convinced of your innocence and pray for your happiness and long life.” The first part of the blessings gave her the desired moral strength, but feeling of long life completely depressed her.

The van left with Mary deeply engrossed in the sweet memories of church life that had made deep impression on her impressionable mind. Her innate desire to help others had endeared her place in the hearts of everyone and made her a darling of all in and around the church till she grew to be a charming girl and was married to a young man of her caste in the same church.

Matrimonial knot that had tied two unknown souls into an alliance of celestial love soon turned out to be a bad gamble and a curse for Mary and John. Unfortunately, there was an inherent divergence in their basic habits which strained their marital relations. Relations that started with a grand flourish of love were soon replaced by hatred. John was an extremely lazy man and devoid of any desire to progress in life. He spent his time in the gang of drunkards and gamblers and would hardly go out for fishing to perform his primary duty of earning livelihood. Mary, on the other hand, had a passion for hard work and an inborn desire to progress in life. For one, laziness was a curse and for the other, it was a blessing and source of happiness. Mary hated the drone for he had landed the family in a state of abject poverty. She tolerated in the beginning but the relations continued to sour. Her dream of a happy married life had been completely shattered into fragments. She often scolded him for his irresponsibility with the fond hope of correcting his bad habits. To save him, John often accused her of her arrogant behaviour and in this web of mutual accusations, their relations got further entangled. In spite of all these vital personality differences, Mary still intensely loved him and could not live without him even for a moment.

"John, why don't you try to conquer your weakness of drinking and gambling? You know, I have a deep-rooted hatred for such habits. I often dream of having a house of our own. We must also save some money to educate our children, so that they don't rot like us. Don't you want to progress in life?"

John put his arms around her neck, looked lovingly into her dreamy eyes and said, "Darling, you know, I love you intensely and just want you to be before my eyes all the time. One day, I will build a beautiful mansion on the sea-shore where you will live like a queen."

Mary also became little soft, lovingly rested her head on his shoulders with eyes riveted in the eyes of John, and said, "I know you love me very much. Love is essential for life, but love alone does not sustain life. Don't build castles in the air. You have to earn for your dreams and for the future of our life also."

"Mary, I do feel a sense of guilt for not looking after you properly. Please excuse me for my laziness. When I see my friends, I forget everything and fall a prey to these vices. I promise I will certainly go to catch fish from tomorrow."

But all promises of John were false and he never changed his despicable designs. When completely under the spell of liquor, he would only say, "Look darling, nature maintains a perfect balance. All are not born to work. There are some who work while others enjoy. In this house also you are there to work and I am born to enjoy. I will start working when you will stop."

Mary had, in fact, grown sick of John's pernicious habits and was fully convinced that he would never learn to work in life. In a fit of emotional frenzy, she ran after him a couple of times with a stick threatening to beat him, the frail looking John being a poor match for her in physical strength. She would, however, be apologetic every time and say, "John dear, I am ashamed of what I did. In fact, I never want to do it. I only wish you to work hard and earn some money." These petty quarrels, exchange of hot words and abuses of Mary became an everyday fun for the neighbours and all arguments had ceased to have any impact on the stubborn John. Her patience was completely exhausted and one day she threatened him with dire consequences.

"Look John! I have been rather too soft with you. You are not behaving like a man. If you do not go for fishing tomorrow, I will throw you into the sea." A heavy dose of liquor resulted in oversleep and John could not go for fishing even if he had a little desire to mend his ways. His unchanged attitude had compelled Mary to finally decide the matter that evening. She was a woman of firm determination and actually meant what she had threatened. When John came home she was sleeping. She was unaware that she had recently conceived. She was unwell and not in a position to go out for fishing. There was nothing to eat in the home. The moment John entered the hut Mary was furious. She had grown sick of the abusive relationship and pounced upon him like a hungry wolf. The volcano finally exploded. Her tongue turned venomous and she was spitting fire. She abused him and hit him with a stick in the presence of the villagers, who only smiled at the fate of poor John.

"You are a compulsive liar and have exceeded all limits of my patience. Today I am not going to leave you. You wretch, you have made my life miserable. I will throw you into the sea. Let the sharks tear you to pieces. I do not want to see your face." Still not satisfied, she chased him to the sea-shore and virtually pushed tipsy John into the sea and came back home. Her action in the heat of that moment proved to be extremely painful in life.

That evening the sea was extremely violent and the rain-god was exceedingly furious. It appeared as if the curses of heaven were about to fall on the people of earth. Torrential rains and her physical condition barred Mary from going to the rough sea to bring back John. She was restless and mentally disturbed. She rolled in her bed the whole night and had not even a wink of sleep. There was none to share her distress and only the sky was her faithful companion in shedding tears, both becoming calm towards the dawn.

John did not return home that night. Mary went to the sea-shore and searched all over the place for his love-life. John was not traceable any where. She ran back to the village and enquired from his glass-mates who were also unable to provide any clue to his whereabouts. Some laughed at her behaviour while others pitied her condition. A few decided to launch a search. The search party came back in the afternoon with John's empty boat.

"Where is my John?" implored the impatient lady.

"Why do you ask us now? You are responsible for his death. You had first thrown him into the stormy sea and then left him at the mercy of the violent waves to be hit by the boulders and now you want to know his whereabouts? We saw his dead body floating in the deep sea, but could not seize it in spite of our best efforts."

Mary was shocked to hear all this. Her ears could not believe and it was as if her heart had stopped beating. She fell down on the ground and on regaining consciousness found herself in the hospital with police around her.

"Come out. We have reached our destination," shouted the policeman on reaching the jail. Mary was suddenly brought back to reality from the reflections of the past.

In the jail, Mary was greeted by the strange inquisitive looks of her future comrades. The inmates looked at her with suspicious eyes. They considered her to be arrogant and a woman of ungracious behaviour who had brutally murdered her husband. They suspected her to be hot-tempered and volatile in nature. They were not aware of the fact that by nature Mary was a sweet-natured, simple and witty girl. She had received good education during her stay in the church and that she was very dynamic and progressive. They were ignorant that Mary was very hard-working, never shirked away from responsibility and displayed maturity beyond her years.

Languishing in jail, Mary hardly talked to anyone in the beginning. She was generally restless and mentally disturbed.

Time seemed to stagnate in distress. Sleep at night in the cell was naturally not possible and her thoughts wandered all over the place. She fluttered like an innocent sparrow put suddenly in a cage. She often thought of John whom she had now lost for ever. Shedding tears of repentance, she would often murmur, "I loved John from the core of my heart… I had none except him in the world…How could I even think of harming him?...Perhaps, I alone was responsible for his death…I am a murderer and God has rightly punished me. I will now atone for my sins here."

The sinking feeling of loneliness of the once chirpy girl had now completely depressed her. She was like a bird fluttering on the ground, whose wings had been mercilessly clipped. There was none to share her pain and she resigned herself to the life of gloomy and stinking prison cells. Empty spaces of the dark and dirty cell stared back at her and sitting in the corner, she would often weep in hiding so that her muffled sobs could not be heard by others. The dazzling lights of the church were replaced by the poorly lit corridors of the jail. Instead of the soft music of the church she was now getting accustomed to the jarring sound of the wooden sticks striking against the metal bars of the cells. She had no option but to face these cruel realities of life and had learnt to compromise with the changed phase of life with insurmountable grit. Faith in destiny and constant study of Bible had made her more philosophical in life.

Time has the marvelous capacity of healing even the deepest wounds. Pain, sufferings, sorrow and privation get lightened even in progression and congregation when one begins to live with them. Mary also soon got accustomed to the agony of life, quickly adapted herself to the jail routine and impressed all by her qualities of hard work and good behaviour. They would often remark, "Mary, you do not appear to have committed any crime. You are such a noble and god-fearing soul that you can never even think of harming any person. Tell us, did you really kill your husband?" She would only respond with a gentle smile and look at the sky. At times when urged to reveal the cause of her conviction, she would only say, "I had committed innumerable crimes. I longed for light while destiny had chosen darkness for me. Unfortunately, I tried to build sand-castle on the turbulent sea-shore and dreamt of living happily in it with my family. Ardent desire for a happy and peaceful life is my greatest crime for which I have been punished". Required to do hard labour in the beginning, the fellow convicts began to share her work and she was soon granted exemption on maternity grounds. With a celestial smile on her dark flushing cheeks and dreamy eyes, she was now normally busy with a ball of yellow yarn and a pair of knitting needles.

The days began to crawl and seven months after her confinement in the jail, Mary gave birth to a son. There was a wave of intense rejoicing all around and the fellow prisoners had an evening of great merriment. Motherhood brought further change in her life and she became a completely different person. For about three years this most valuable creation of God inhaled the prison air. For his better future and proper upbringing Mary decided to send him to the church. The intensity of emotional stress on such partings cannot be easily fathomed. She had to crucify her motherly instinct in order to provide decent education to her son and also ensure that he remained ignorant about her mother and was not dubbed as the son of a murderer. At times she longed to see him but had to be contended only with occasional postal information from the church. She often wrote to Father to ensure that her son inculcated values of love, truth, honesty and hard work. She desired him to be a good human being in life.

Years rolled by and Mary had gone grey, less because of age and more because of the burden of uncommitted sin that she carried in her heart. In spite of the comparatively good food now served in the jail and better means of entertainment, particularly for those who had earned a name for their better behaviour, Mary continued to grow weak and the natural glow and innocent smile had completely withered from her once ever-smiling face. Separation from husband, whom she missed beyond measures, had been partially replaced by the birth of the son whose absence had now totally drained her of all physical energies and she had little desire to live. She would hardly join an entertainment session and rarely watched the TV.

One evening, propelled perhaps by a providential urge, she joined the band of TV lovers. That evening photograph of a notorious smuggler was being repeatedly telecast on the TV who had escaped from police custody while being taken for medical examination and later on landed in police net at the airport. His name was Habib. The moment Mary saw the photograph she cried, "The name is wrong. The name is wrong. He is John. He is John, my husband."

"But his name is Habib," remarked an astonished co-prisoner.

"No, he is certainly John. He cannot be Habib."

Some comrades laughed at her reaction and thought she had gone mad because of the excessive mental tension. Mary ran towards the office to see the warden who was unfortunately not available. She was extremely restless at night and could not have a wink of sleep. The photo of

John repeatedly flashed before her eyes. "How could it be?" she wondered. "John had died years back...He might have not died. The other fishermen might have given the wrong information to her and also to the court...But why should they do all this?...May be the photograph was not that of John. May be she was mistaken." With all these mixed feelings, there was still a glimmer of hope in her heart.

Next day she got ready a little earlier and went to the warden who took her to the jailor.

"Sir, yesterday night I saw the photograph of a smuggler telecast on the TV. It was that of John, my husband," said an anxious Mary.

The jailor first looked at the warden with astonishment and then at Mary. He was rather furious. "Are you in your senses? You know you had killed your husband years back. You must have seen his ghost. Has he come out of the grave now?"

"I do not know how to convince you, sir. It looks a mystery to me too but he was certainly John. I cannot make a mistake in recognising my husband. There was only one difference. His moustache was thicker in the photograph and he was also supporting a French beard."

The jailor was suddenly reminded that the photograph of the smuggler had also been published in the newspaper. He quickly located the same and placed it before Mary.

"Do you recognise him?"

"Exactly sir, he is John. He is my John. He is alive."

Her assertion was so far being taken lightly but it deserved serious consideration now. The jailor changed his tone and politely remarked, "Go and attend to your work. We will try to find out the details and let you know."

Mary stood for a few seconds and then left the chamber with a mixture of hope and despair. The jailor got more keenly interested in the case because Mary had been convicted for the murder of her husband who, according to her, was alive. He wanted to probe into the assertion of Mary and collected more details about Habib. Mary completely forgot about her conviction and imprisonment and the excitement of meeting John now began to build in her mind. Every morning while crossing, she would stand before the warden, look at him inquisitively but would get nothing but disappointment. The warden would silently pass without conveying anything.

One cloudy morning after rains, the warden came to Mary and sprang a surprise. "Habib, whose photograph you saw on the TV, has been sent to this very jail. He arrived last night. Would you like to meet him?"

Mary could not believe her ears. There was an unusual glow of joy and surprise on her face which unfortunately soon withered away. She became serious. "What will be the use of meeting John? He may fail to recognise me, or may purposely refuse to accept me as his wife. Where shall I go if I am released? I shall not be able to call Sunny from the church. He will now be called the son of a smuggler."

She was deeply engrossed in these thoughts when the warden suddenly shattered the calm and shouted, "Would you come with me or not?"

"Yes I will." replied Mary with a deep sense of authority and simultaneously nodded her head vigorously in affirmative. She instantly followed the warden.

After passing through the dark and desolate corridors, the warden stopped in front of a cell and pointed towards a man whose back was towards the gate of the cell. Mary hesitatingly stood for a few moments, the heart beating violently in her bosom. Courage seemed to be failing within her. She retraced her steps and thought of going back. After a little introspection, her steps stopped. She looked at the warden and perhaps more to avoid being called a liar than prompted by the desire to meet John, she said with a lump in her throat, "John!" Her feeble voice could have been hardly heard by the man in the cell who naturally remained absolutely unmoved.

Mary cleared her throat and said more loudly, "John, please see who is here?"

The man looked back from the corner of his shoulder, stared at the caller but again turned back his face. The warden, who was observing impatiently, stepped forward and said, "Habib!"

A man of thin and lean built, dressed in jeans and T-shirt got up and said, "Yes, what can I do for you?"

"This lady wants to talk to you."

"Yes madam."

"John!"

"Excuse me, my name is Habib."

"You may be Habib for the whole world but you are John for me," said Mary with confidence.

"Are you crazy? I said my name is Habib."

Though the man posed to display a sense of determination, a peculiar state of nervousness was conspicuous on his face and tiny drops of perspiration were clearly discernable on his forehead.

"John, I am Mary, your wife. For God sake, tell them that you are John. I have already suffered enough and have missed you beyond measures during all these years," implored Mary.

The man stepped forward, came closer to Mary, perhaps to have a look at the person who had called him by his real name after so many years. To her utter amazement his John was standing right in front of her. Mary could not control herself and began to cry. Without uttering a word, John placed his cold hands on the warm fingers of the woman who was holding the iron bars of the cell. It was as if time had come to a standstill for Mary. John peeped into her eyes to trace the youthful charms of his Mary but could only find a pale and passive woman with grey hair completely broken in body and spirit. Glancing slowly from top to bottom, he was suddenly shocked to see her in a convict's dress.

"But why are you putting on this dress?"

"John, have you recognised me?"

"Tell me what crime have you committed?"

"I became a victim of time."

"I can't understand this enigma."

"I had murdered my husband."

"Your husband?"

"Yes my husband, Mr. John D'Souza."

"But you never murdered me. I am alive. Why should you be convicted for not committing a crime?"

"All this was the curse of Providence."

"All this is mystery to me. I can't understand what you are saying. Please tell me the truth. What have you done?"

"I told you. This was His command." Briefly she narrated the story of her conviction.

"No Mary. Why blame God for our own misdeeds. I curse the moment I deserted you."

"It is not your fault John. We are all slaves of such unfortunate times. In a fit of emotional frenzy I lost the balance of my mind and failed to temper my hostile behaviour. A moment makes a mistake and the whole life suffers. Alas! We could only learn to wait, think at that moment and allow our tempers to cool down."

"You have become too philosophical," said John with a little smile on his face.

"No, I am only beginning to see the reality of life little more clearly."

"You will be set free now. You will be able to go back to the village with all the fortune that I have amassed during all these years."

"Burn all your fortune to ashes. I never wanted you to be a traitor and earn by anti-social means. You forgot John, only proper means justify proper ends. I will prefer to remain poor, live by your honest meager earnings, and live in a small hut with my son than be cursed as the wife of a smuggler."

"Son?"

"Yes, your own son."

"But where is he?"

"He is in the church."

"Oh! Mary. How much have you been wronged because of me?"

"Don't say this, John. Thank God. All our days of misfortune shall be over soon. Once time snatched you from me, today I have snatched you from time. Storm will wither one day, Father had predicted. I will go, bring back Sunny and make a good hut for us to live in. Our home shall be the abode of honest and hard-working people."

After the night-long rains, the clouds that had shadowed the sun had withered. The corridors of the jail were now beginning to be brighter and sunlight falling directly on John's face was unfolding the existence of a latent determination. The rays of future hope were glistening in the dark sunken eyes of Mary and were getting reflected in those of John. The lips were perfectly motionless but the hearts were conveying more than the words.

Dressed in bright coloured skirt with hair decoratively tied in a bun with a rose from the prison garden tucked in, she was impatiently waiting for the arrival of the warden. "Mrs. Mary D'Souza, come with me to the office. We have to complete some legal formalities," said the waiting warden and Mary unwillingly followed.

Mary slowly dragged her feet forward with her heart pulling her back. Strange are the ways of destiny. On one stormy morning when she wanted John to stay with her, he deserted her. Today on a bright morning when again she wanted to be with John, she was being forced to leave him. Once she wanted to be out of the murky jail and cursed the day she was thrown in, today she wanted to stay in the jail with John but was being pushed out. In the grip of past and future, she saw the present slipping quickly from her hands. John called her back and promised "Mary, please forgive me. I assure you I will go for fishing everyday and will earn for all of you by honest means. Tell the truth to our son and educate him properly. When the storm comes again, we shall meet on the sea-shore and shall live happily ever after." Waiting for a moment, he remarked, "Mary you are looking stunningly charming. I love you." She blew a flying kiss and departed with a heavy heart.